Acknowledgements

I would like to thank my partner and immediate family for giving me encouragement and enthusiasm whilst writing this book.

Especially Justin Bowles who has been my right hand man I could not have done this without him.

Mr Pathak, Orthopedic consultant at the Fitzwilliam Hospital Peterborough for his Medical expertise.

Emma, Physiotherapist.

My friends for their enthusiasm.

Chapter 1

It was the final day of the golf tournament at Trout Valley Golf Club.
Ross's tournaments took him all over the world.
Although to be in Africa it felt something special.
Not just for the golf but also for the wonderful views of,
Mountain scenery and the wild life animals.
The open spaces gave him a feeling of freedom.
It felt like a different world.
What a lovely sight to see on his way to the Golf Hotel.
Giraffes with their long necks buried in the tree top eating,
the leaves on the trees.
Impala's running away from a group of elephants strolling,
towards a water hole.
There were many more species to see along the way.
Ross would say when you visit Africa you leave the,
Ordinary life behind.

Ross jumped out of bed knocking the alarm clock off,
the bed side table.
'God look at the time I'm supposed to be on the first tee,
At 8-30, he said talking to himself.
Ross peered out the window the clouds were clearing,
The morning mist was lifting on the lake.
It was going to be another hot sunny day.
'Ouch oh shit that's a bloody good start to the day',
He said hitting his toe on the edge of the bed.
'That's all I need, and to be late today of all days'

Ross was rushing around giving himself a talking too.

 'Right calm down'

He did some calming breathing to take the tension away.

He made himself a cup of coffee, then freshened up and,

Quickly shaved.

After he was dressed he decided to phone Jimmy.

The phone seemed to ring for ages.

Typical knowing him, Ross thought, bet he's still in bloody bed.

Jimmy picked up the phone.

What's the matter? Jimmy asked Ross.

'I was just wondering if you were up.'

'I missed the alarm.'

 'Course I am, stop panicking Jimmy replied.

''Right I'll be ready in a few minutes' replied Ross.

  He looked down at his feet.

Bugger it' he cursed to himself 'I've got odd socks on'.

He quickly looked for the other matching sock.

Wondering what else would go wrong.

He had no time for breakfast.

They would have to grab some fruit from the restaurant to eat on their, way to the course.

He knew he should have left Jimmy at the bar on his own last night, and had an early night.

 Late night drinking didn't do any of them any favours.

  Jimmy was too busy chatting up the bar attendant at midnight.

 Asking her, would she like a lesson getting the ball out the sand, bunkers?

   Ross didn't think that was the only thing on Jimmy's mind.

More like get her in the bunker.

He kept reminding Jimmy how late it was, and of the final day ahead.
"Come on Jimmy no more drinks' Ross told him.
'It's the big day tomorrow'.
'Time you'd had enough'.
'Got to get your beauty sleep lads' said the barmaid.
Jimmy winked at her.
'You can join me if you like?'
I'll ignore that remark' she replied crossly.
'Sorry didn't mean to offend you' 'I'm only joking' replied Jimmy.
'Yeah well off you go you two' replied the barmaid.
Jack the lad that's what some of the players called him.
Jimmy's life consisted of three things.
Golf, drink, and women, in that order he would say.
Ross had got him out off a few scrapes in his time.
He knew he shouldn't have taken any notice of Jimmy ordering,
another round of drinks that late at night.
Ross was annoyed with himself, for listening to him in the first place.
He needed to be in good form for the final day.
Then Jimmy's his best friend.
They had many fun nights out together.
Especially down the local pub playing snooker the competition was,
there.
They would be there late at night seeing who could win the last,
frame of snooker.
The landlord who say in a friendly tone' haven't you two got any,
homes to go to.'

They would reply I suppose it's chucking out time then Frank.

'Better call it a night', 'time we went home' Ross would say.

They would stagger out the pub, hoping they didn't see a policeman, around that time of night.

 Then Jimmy would say to Ross, 'you can't go home in that state'.

'Your mum wouldn't be very pleased with me if I let you drive home, worse for wear'.

'You had better stay at mine'.

 But then Ross knew he would end up at Jimmy's.

 All Jimmy had done since he arrived at the hotel besides golfing was, to chat up the female staff he was crafty at worming his way around, them.

At meal times he would ask for extras on the side.

Ross would give him a kick on his shins under the table 'what's that for' Jimmy would ask?

''You know very well' Ross would comment, all Jimmy would do was, laugh it off you've no sense of, humour he would say to Ross, not your sort was the reply from Ross.

'You're too serious sometimes that's your problem 'Jimmy would say,

'The trouble with you Jimmy is you don't take things serious enough, sometimes when you should' commented Ross.

 'What do you mean by that' ask Jimmy,

Ross gave him a stern, look 'forget it was his reply.

Chapter 2

The hotel was set in a stunning area overlooking mountains, and lakes, the gardens were full of flowering shrubs all in bloom.
The Acacia trees were mesmerizing how they grew flat across the top, of the tree you knew you were in Africa.
There was just something about being there that was captivating,
The hotel grounds had several lodges overlooking the golf course full, of quest that had come to see the players in the tournament.
The golf course was well maintained.
A tree lined course with some tight fairways and immaculate greens.
It had picturesque water hazards there were rocks lining some of the, fairways, and there were ravines that must be carried to the finish of, the hole, all over the course grew wild orchids.
Whilst the bushes where teem with bird life.
The staff were friendly and always made that extra special welcome to, all.
The rooms had that freshness feel to them inside.
Spacious with lake views from the balcony.
There were bowls carved out of wood placed around the room and, beautiful pictures of animals on the wall.
The foyer in the hotel had marble floors.
In the lounging area there was a large big brick fire place.
There was plenty of seating area outside where people could sit and, take in the views.
What better relaxed atmosphere could you have?
With a meal and a drink, good friends what more could you ask for.
The fishing lakes drew a lot of young people they were full of trout, fish.
Families enjoyed their time out boating on the lakes.
The young lads would come in all excited and shouting about their, catch that day.
Whilst holding up a big trout fish.

If they wanted the chef would cook the trout for them to eat whilst, they were at the hotel or they could take their trout fish home.
The sun going down at night over the mountains was a stunning sight, to see.
Ross would lean on the balcony and watch the sun sinking slowly, down to earth.
The stillness of the moonlight ripples on the water was breathtaking, taking and tranquil.
You could feel the call of the mountains as you looked out in the, distance.
It felt so peaceful If only he could put this moment of time in a bottle, and carry it with him.
The tournament was a big event Ross desperately wanted to win.
There were three players besides him on the leader board with the, same points lead.
Ross knew he was in with a chance to lift the cup.
 Rushing around grabbing some fruit to eat on the way was not going, down too well with him.
Jimmy also had a competitive edge to the final day.
Ross knew he had to focus his mind only on the game ahead.
This was the shortest game Ross used to say.
It's between the ears.
Ross shouted to his caddy.
'Hey Dill are the clubs in the golf cart'?
"And don't forget my shoes.
'Yes boss' answered caddy Dill.
'What would I do without you asked Ross?'
Dill shrugged his shoulders.
Oh those shoes they were his pride and joy.
With his logo on they looked quite jazzy.
He had them especially made.
The players would say Ross is here they knew by the shoes in the, changing room.
Dill knew what Ross was like when he was annoyed
He'd worked the longest of all Ross's caddy but could not explain why.

He knew Ross had a soft side to him and also knew when not to say,
anything.

The clubs were in the golf cart and they were on their way,
to the course.

The cart was speeding down the drive pulling up sharp on the graveled,
area.

Jimmy was behind him with his caddy. 'Go on you two, 'get signed in,
shouted Dill.

They both went rushing through the club house door.

They signed in and made their way to the first tee.

"Phew that was close' said Ross to Jimmy'

"Yes sorry Ross I should have listened to you' admitted Jimmy.

"Yeah well let's concentrate on the game ahead shall we' suggested,
Ross.

The last thing he wanted was for Jimmy to go on about the night,
before.

Making all the excuses he could for a late night drinking.

"Right no more jabbering' said Dill 'time to play your game.'

They walked on to the first tee.

The crowds were gathering around the fenced off area to watch them,
take their first drive of the day.

Ross looked up to the sky it was bright blue.

Looks like it's going to be a good day he said to Dill.

Well let's hope it end that way' Dill said.

One of the ground staff walked along side them on the course.

Carrying a placard board showing Ross and Jimmy's also the other,
two player's names on with their up to date scores of the game he,
would be following them around the course.

This would give the people in the crowd some idea who was in the,
lead.

Dill took out the golf club from the bag handed it to Ross.

A driver he loved the feel of the club.

A good strike of the ball it would fly a good distance down the,
fairway.

He did a few exercises to get his body flexed and relaxed.

Took a few practice swings with the club,

Ross had strong muscles it was all down to his training he did daily in, the gym.

He was ready the adrenalin had kicked in.

"Keep your cool said Dill"

"Remember you're the only one out there in your mind."

Jimmy took his time talking to his caddy big Joe.

nicknamed for his height 6tf 4 and big muscles.

Joe spent all his spare time in the gym.

He wore bright coloured trousers with a diamond pattern.

He used to say to Jimmy that no one would miss seeing them on the, course.

Jimmy stood only 5ft 6inches he looked like a dwarf standing next to, Joe.

Ross would sometimes say to Jimmy, there's only one lot of exercise, on your mind.

Several players had already teed off.

Ross knew Jeff Daniels and Billy Hopkins were two shots ahead on, the leader score board.

Jeff Daniels took a few practice swings with his driver.

He waited for the starter to introduce him on the tee.

After the introductions was over.

He hit his shot, whoosh it went down the fairway.

'Sounded good to me' said his caddy.

Jeff smirked I'll take that he commented.

Ross knew there were some big hitters out there.

The starter picks up the microphone and announced, to the crowd.

All the way from England', 'Ross Portland'.

The crowd acknowledged him.

Ross tipped his hat to acknowledge them.

He took his stance then hit the ball.

It flew down the fairway past the first bunker.

The crowd roared shouting out great shot.

Ross stepped back raised his hand to thank them.

Then it was Jimmy's turn the starter announced.

"On the tee we have Jimmy Day also from England."

The crowd turned their heads as some girls shouted.

'Good luck Jimmy.'

Jimmy just smiled and acknowledged the crowd.

He took his stance swung the club hitting the ball.

Slicing his drive to the right it landed in some trees.

Someone from the crowd roared' oh my god he's in the trees'.

Jimmy wasn't very pleased with himself.

Before handing the club back to Big Joe to put in the golf bag.

He hit the ground hard with it.

'No good getting like that Jimmy 'said Joe.

'This is the first shot of the day'.

'Just control your temper'.

Jimmy just walked off ahead.

Looks like we're going to have some fun today though Joe.

Joe knew it would take Jimmy a few holes to calm down.

But then Joe wasn't the sort of person to put up with Jimmy's, nonsense for too long.

He would soon give him a talking too in a nice way.

The next two players were introduced and took their shot.

After all the players had tee'd off on the first hole.

They walked down the fairway together until they got to where their, ball laid then proceeded to take their second shoot,

Jimmy walked towards the trees looking for his ball.

"Here it is' said big Joe.

The ball was in thick bramble you could just identify Jimmy's name, marked on the ball as it lay there.

By that time the rules attendant had come over in his buggy.

He looked to see what position the ball lay.

He had a discussion with Jimmy and his caddy.

They knew the ball was unplayable and Jimmy would have to take a, drop.

That would mean Jimmy would be playing for an extra shot on his, score of the hole.

He was none too happy with that.

Big Joe turned to Jimmy handed him the golf club and gave him a pep, talk.

Jimmy was still cursing himself for having a bad start to the game.

He knew all he could do was to get the ball back on the fairway.

He took his stance and hit the ball striking it well.

"That's it' said Joe 'good shot."

After Several more holes, Ross had settled in to his game.

He loved the challenge of the course.

'Keep your cool and you'll be ok 'said Dill.

'Don't try any fancy shots.

There were some short holes to play with several bunkers around them.

They were deep bunkers with thick layers of sand in them.

If the ball got buried in one of them you could be showered,

With sand trying to hit the ball out of the bunker and on to,

the green.

Ross knew some of the other players were doing well.

Mind game that's what he'd say to Dill.

'And it's what happens on the day' would be Dills reply.

'We don't want any repeats of last year's tournament',

'When you gave it away to Brin all because you double,

Bogged the first two holes' commented Dill.

'Don't remind me what a disastrous day that was' Replied Ross.

Ross could feel the heat from the sun on his brow.

Dill took the bottle of water from the bag and passed it to Ross.

'Here you need to have a sip of water Ross' he said.

'Can't have you getting lethargic in all this heat'

'Phew it's hotter today than yesterday replied Ross.

Ross took a sip and passed the bottle back to Dill then wiped, his brow.

The peak from his cap may have shaded a certain amount of sun, from his face.

But in Africa it could get much hotter on the course than in other, country's he had been to.

'At least it's not raining' he said to Dill.

Not like when we played in Scotland.

It rained on and off all four days and the wind nearly blew you away.

Chapter 3

Ross caught a glimpse of his mum dad and Sister Josie,
in the crowd.
They had flown over for the tournament a day earlier.
So as they could have some time with Ross in the evening.
Mary, Ross's Mum was looking forward to seeing her son.
She enjoyed watching him play.
Knowing golf was his greatest passion.
The four of them had arranged to meet for a meal in the evening.
They all sat around the table discussing the hotel accommodation.
Josie beckoned to Ross to pass her a menu asking,
'What's the special of the day'?
'Lamb that's what's on the menu' replied Ross.
'Or you can have the special worm' he said smiling.
'A worm what are you talking about' asked Josie.
'Mopane worm' replied Ross.
It's considered a delicacy in Africa.
'Crunchy like potato chips' he carried on saying.
'It can boost your protein and is highly nutritious'
'Add a bit of chilli it will do you the power of good.
When you have eaten it you get a certificate''.
Ross tried hard to keep a straight face.
'Well you can eat it if you like I'm definitely not eating it not bloody,
likely' answered Josie.
She had a sour look on her face.
'Anyway I'm not that desperate to get a certificate just by eating a,
worm' she commented.
Josie's body shivered with the thought of it all.

Phillip laughed and winked at Ross.

'Think I will stick to the Lamb and you two can stop the smirking', said Josie.

'Now then children' commented Mary, let not spoil the evening just, order your meals'.

Ross had heard that comment many times in his younger days.
He replied yes mum.'

Phillip, Mary and Josie all enjoyed their meal together with Ross.

After their meal they took an evening stroll down by the lakes to, admire the beautiful view of the sunset shimmering reflection on the, lake.
It was like fire in the sky.

This was what family life was all about thought Mary as they strolled, around the grounds.
Time together.

Ross lived in a beautiful lavish house on the edge of town down a, long narrow tree lined road with fields around.

There was a farm house at the top of the lane, the farmer,
often waved to Ross when he was ploughing the fields.

Ross loved nothing more than to take a stroll down the lane on a, Sunday morning when he was not on tour.

He would sit on a bench half way down the road, and take in the, fresh air, listening to the rustle of the trees in the breeze and hearing, the birds singing in the tree tops.

Across the fields there were woodlands, sometimes he would walk, the, bridle path it was so peaceful.

Then he would be off to the local pub to meet Jimmy for a pint and, Sunday lunch.

What more could you ask for he though.

There were only a few houses built in that area Ross liked,
the privacy.

Many a girl took a fancy to him especially his good looks,
and charm.

In fact Ross had several girlfriends but he knew the right one had,
not come along yet.

He kept his head.

He wondered sometime if they were just after a lavish easy life style.

Ross's parents lived the other side of town.

His dad Phillip didn't like to miss the final day of the golf tournament,
if he got the opportunity to be there.

He was proud of his son's achievement.

He always encouraged Ross to play other sports.

Golf was his favorite sport when he was growing up.

Ross would put some canes in the ground and make a frame with,
some old sheets.

Using it as a practice area hitting the balls so hard the sheet would fall,
to the ground.

Ross would swear hoping his mother wasn't close enough to hear him.

His dad just laughed until his side's ached.

Josie would say he was stupid she knew it wouldn't work.

"I'll tell mum you were swearing 'she would say.

Ross would shout at her "You do if you dare"

He would swing his club in the air.

Then he would chase her around the garden and pull her hair.

"Ouch she would shout out loud"

Running into the house crying to her mother saying 'he hurt me he,
pulled my hair'.

Ross would argue' its'all her fault."

They would both get a talking to.

Mary didn't want to hear another word from either of them.

The memories brought tears to their eyes with laughter.

Josie his sister was 4 years younger than Ross and,
they were very close.

He was very protective towards her when she was growing up.

Ross knew Josie was always there for their parents.

This took the pressure of him.

Especially as he was on tour a lot.

Phillip had a heart attack a year ago and was lucky to be alive.

He ran his own business selling motor cars.

 Mary had worked in the office before Phillip's heart attack.

 Phillip employed another sales manager.

 The stress of it all had taken its toll on Mary.

They decided to employ someone to take over from her.

 They lived in a four bedroom house on the edge of town.

 That over looked the woodland area.

They liked the quietness and the privacy.

 Mary had decorated the house herself.

  She was good at knowing what colour's would coordinate in,
   each room.

  Josie would say 'you have wasted your talent mum'.

'You should have been an interior designer.'

   Phillip enjoyed his time in the garden when he was not working at,
the car showroom.

  He prided himself on his lawns paying special attention to the,
boarders.

 He would warn Ross not to chip on the front lawn.

 He had plenty of space around the back of the house at the bottom,
off the garden which was covered in grass.

 Ross felt guilty sometimes knowing he wasn't always there for his,
dad.

 His life revolved around his golf.

 Knowing he had to live his life.

 His parents would not want it any other way.

  'Don't you worry about us'? They would say.

'Life's too short you have to do what you want to do'.

It's your life so live it' Mary would say to them.

 Josie was content with being around her mum and dad.

 She was more a home bird not really interested in travelling;

Beside she had her business to run.

Her mum would remind her about how hard her dad had worked and of,
his heart attack.

She did not want Josie to spend every hour in the shop.

 All work and no play she would say to her.

Josie prided herself how far she had got in life.
Ross had not been the only successful one in the family.
  But then Ross was very proud of his sister.
He would tell the lads if ever you need to send someone special a,
Bouquet of flowers, he knew just the right person to contact.
His sister Josie;
  Josie had worked hard putting in all the hours in a day she could to,
get the business off the ground.
 Her mum would say to her 'it will take time.
 But you will get there in the end'.
 Underneath she knew Josie was a determined woman.
Nothing was going to stop her succeeding in life.

Chapter 4

Josie lived in a flat above the florist shop she owned in town.
Small but perfect for her.
The shop had the old curiosity charm to it.
With wooden floor boards, which she liked.
They added character to the building.
When you walked in it made you feel as though you could spend all,
day in there.
Browsing the shelves for little knick knacks.
Josie had a flair for making it come alive, always paying special,
attention to the display of flowers in the shop window.
She stood some boxes in a corner of the shop and made a pretty fairy,
garden with some lanterns to brighten it up.
The children loved to admire the fairies and elves.
They loved the houses, toad stools around the plants.
'How pretty' the girls used to say.'
They didn't want to leave.
In the end some mothers would buy items to allow their daughters to,
make their own garden.
"We can make one when we get home" their daughters would say.
Josie saw the excitement in their eye's at having their own fairy,
garden.
Rushing to get home to plan where they were going to put them.
'Send me a picture' Josie would always ask them'.
'Then I can put it in the shop' she would tell them.
That encouraged them more with their own little fantasy.

Josie would be asked to demonstrate flower arranging for the, women's institute especially at Christmas time.
The ladies would try their hand at making a Christmas wreath.
Josie would judge the best one and present the winner a prize.
The competition between the ladies was very competitive.

Josie would spend most of her time in trousers and tops.
But when she put on a dress she looked stunning.
She was a pretty brunette with a slender figure.
Many men had asked her out.
Her last boyfriend got a bit too possessive.
She wasn't having any of that she would say.
A mummy's boy he was always quizzing her, wanting to know where, she had been.
He didn't like it if she stopped off at her mum and dad's.
He would get angry with her if she was late home from having a drink, with her friends.
He expected a meal on the table when he came in at any time of day.
He was also a lazy sod.
Many times she would go around picking up his washing that he'd, flung on the bedroom floor.
Also leaving a sink full of dirty pots soaking in a bowl of water, overnight for her to come down to the next morning and see them, floating in scum for her to wash up.
That really annoyed Josie.
Don't forget to wash up she would shout down to him when she went, up to bed.
She knew bloody well she would be wasting her breath.
At one time she was so mad when he had left the pots in a bowl of, water over night.
She thought I'll teach him with his dirty habits.
So the next morning she got up early.
She filled his flask with the dish water.
He'll get a shock, when he goes to pour it thinking it's full of tea' she, thought to herself.
Serves himself right.

~ 19 ~

When he came in from work that evening he threw a tantrum.

Shouting and swearing at Josie.

'You made me look a right fucking fool at work today 'he said to Josie.

'Why's that' asked Josie with a smile on her face.

'You know bloody well what you did' snapped her partner.

'Filling the flask with the bloody dish water.'

The men took the piss out of me all day.

His face was red with anger.

Josie looked him straight in the eye.

She was not going to be put down by him or any man. 'Serve's you, bloody right' commented Josie.

'I asked you many a time not to leave the pots in soak overnight', Said Josie 'It's not hygienic'.

'I don't like to come down and see them floating in a bowl of dirty, water.'

'It's disgusting'.

'Laziness if you ask me'.

'You couldn't even be bothered to wash them up'.

'I have a business to run' she snapped.

'I don't need to be carrying you also'.

'You're worse than looking after a child'.

Josie was waiting for him to reply.

He stood there with a stunned look on his face and open mouth.

He never expects this from Josie.

She was just about to walk away, she paused a second.

Then she turned to face him.

''Oh and if you think I'm here to run around after you.

You can forget it.'

She had not been born to fetch and carry for any man.

She was his partner not his mother.

If she had to do everything she may just as well live on her own.

Josie calmly walked away.

She knew he had to go and go he did.

One Friday night he was still going on about the dish water in the flask.
 They had a blazing row she picked his clothes up off the floor.
 Opened the window of the flat, and slung them out on to the drive.
 'Piss off back to your mum' she said.
 'Let her run around after you because I'm not anymore'.
 'And if she comes around here I'll put her in her place 'exclaimed,
Josie.
 ' It's a shame she didn't think of what you would be like when,
you're grown up, all that pampering' she said to him in her temper.
 He grabbed his car keys off the hall table.
 Rushed down the stair and outside to his car.
 Josie slammed the door shut behind him.
 She waited in anticipation to see if he was going to,
Knock on the door.
 He quickly collected up his clothes and bundled them in his car.
Shouting to her 'I'll be back later for my other belonging's'.
 Josie leaned out the window 'Don't bother' she shouted back.
 'I'll have them boxed up and sent to your mummies'.
 Then she heard the car start and off he drove.
 Revving the engine and skidding out the drive he was off like a bat out,
of hell.
 She could hear the screeching of tyre's at the corner of the road.
'Good riddance' she thought to herself.
'I think I've had a lucky escape, wondering who the next fool would be,
to get involved with him.
Then she had a good laugh about it.

Josie decided to phone her mum.

The line was engaged, she was wondering who her mum would be, talking to on the phone.

She tried again half hour later.

The phone rang several times before Mary answered.

'Hello mum 'said Josie.

'I tried phoning you earlier but the line was engaged'.

'Yes I know I was talking to Ross' her mum told her.

'He phoned to see how we are and to say he would be home next, week' she told her.

'That's good' said Josie

'Then asked her, what are your plans for tomorrow?

'I haven't made any why' replied Mary.

'Well I thought I would pick you up and take you for afternoon tea.

'Unless you and dad have other plans' Josie asked her.

'No I've nothing arranged' her mum replied.

'Your dad will be in the garden all day you know what he's like' commented Mary.

'He'll stand there all day watching the runner beans grow and waiting, for the tomatoes to turn red'.

Josie laughed.

'Well I'll pick you up at 2'oclock Mum,

'Fine by me look forward to it see you then' replied Mary.

Josie walked into the kitchen rinsed her coffee cup out.

Placed it in the dishwasher then went for a shower.

She could feel the tension easing from her shoulders as the hot water, fell around her neck.

When she had finished showering she patted her skin dry.

Wrapped the towel around her body and made her way to the bedroom.

Flinging herself on the bed, she lay there staring at the ceiling.

What a day she thought to herself.

Never mind tomorrows another day.

Chapter 5

The afternoon tea outing was going down well with,
Josie and her mum.
  Although Mary felt something wasn't quite right.
 Intuition she would say.
  She placed her cup on the saucer looked straight at Josie.
 The curiosity had got the better of her.
 'Josie' she said to her' you can fool people some of the time',
  'not your own mother'.
What's the matter?'
'Nothing should there be' answered Josie.
 Her face turned red.
  ''I know something's not right so don't give me that nothing,
answer' commented Mary'
'Alright mum' replied Josie'.
'If you must know I've kicked him out.
 'What happened? I thought you two were getting on alright' said Mary.
 Josie gave her mum a running commentary on what had happened.
Mary had a job to keep a straight face.
'Well I never thought you would do something like that', she told Josie.
 'It's like this mum if I have to do everything myself I may as well live
on my own' she told her.
'I've done it once so I can do it again'.
 'Anyway it's finished and good riddance to him'.
 'Now let's leave it at that mum and enjoy the rest of the day'.
 'If you say so Josie as long as you are alright that's all that matters'.
  'After all I am your mother I still worry about you no matter how old
you are'.
 'You will understand one day when you have children of your own.'
'Don't bank on it' replied Josie.
 With that Mary didn't say another word about it all.

They both finished their afternoon tea.

Josie looked at her watch.

'What time is it' asked her mum?

'4-45pm Mum' Josie replied.

'I suppose we had better be off 'her mum said.

'Your dad will want his evening meal'

'Well you know what he's like mum he always say's a way to a man's, heart is through his stomach'.

With that Josie paid the bill and they were both heading for the door.

'Thank you Josie for the meal, it's been a lovely afternoon in spite of, what's happened 'said her Mum.

'Yes I enjoyed it also we should do it more often' replied Josie.

With that they gave each other a hug and were on their way.

Josie swung the car in to the drive.

She could see her dad watching out the window.

'See he's waiting for you' said Josie.

Her mum laughed' waiting for his meal more like' she said.

'Hi dad' shouted Josie as she walked in to the hall.

'Ready for your meal' she said laughing.

'Don't be cheeky young lady you're not too big to put across my, knee' he said winking at her'.

'I'd like to see you try' commented Josie.

She gave him a peck on the cheek.

'Got to go I'll phone you later. '

With that they all said their goodbyes.

Mary set to work in the kitchen preparing the evening meal.

Josie enjoyed going out with the girls and spending time, with her family.

Ross was on tour a lot and didn't get home much between, his games.

When he was at home he was in the pub catching up with his mates.

She knew that Ross was happy when he was on the tours with Jimmy.

They were good mates together.

Although Ross had warned her about Jimmy's flirting with the ladies.

Ross didn't want Josie to get hurt.

'Jimmy's not the type of man for you' Ross would comment to Josie.

Josie would say to Ross, 'don't worry about me

I can take care of myself when it comes to men'.

The times Ross would phone home and would give details about their, nights out.

It was not always what his mum wanted to hear.

She would ask him to be careful, especially when he drove home, after a night out drinking'.

Ross used to say.

'I'm a big boy mum I've grown out of short trousers' then would, laugh.

Mary would say to Phillip' no matter how old Josie and Ross were, she still missed their laughter around the house'.

Phillip would answer' well they all have to grow up some time.' knowing what Mary meant.

The house was that quiet some days you could hear a pin drop.

But then Phillip liked no more than to sit in the sun lounge reading his, paper, when he was not down the showroom.

He would go through each article on every page.

Mary would joke and say' it would be bed time before she got to read, it.'

Chapter 6

All that was going through Ross and Jimmy's heads was the game.

They both knew they stood a chance to hold the cup.

Although Ross knew there were some big hitters out there.

Ross took his stance on the 11th tee.

After a couple of practice swings.

He lined up and took his shot.

The ball flew right down the middle of the fairway.

"Great shot" said Dill.

"I'll take that "replied Ross.

Then it was Jeff Daniels turn.

He took his stance; he knew it was a long par five right to left with a, water hazard and two deep bunkers either side of the green.

He hit the ball, it landed in the lake.

'Fuck it 'he said to his caddy.

That's going to bugger up the score card.

Being a Scot's man he was none too pleased with his shot.

After all the other players used to say, he was born with a club in his, hand.

Next was Billy Hopkins who was always very serious on the course.

When he was off the course, just like Jimmy he liked a drink and, laugh.

He took his shot and it landed next to Ross's.

Ross smiled but underneath his smile he felt the tension.

Jimmy nodded walked on to the tee and lined up to take his shot.

Looking down the fairway, he hit the ball, whoosh; it went straight, down the middle past Ross's shot.

He'd out driven Ross.

He looked pleased with himself.

He turned to look at the crowd as a couple of young ladies in short, skirts waved to him.

They were shouting out to him "Jimmy Jimmy we love you."

That put a smile on Jimmy's face.

After all, what could be better than a pretty smile?

Keep your mind on your game commented his caddy Big Joe.

As they walked down the fairway together Ross turned to Jimmy.

"Who are the ladies?"He asked

"No idea "replied Jimmy.

"Looks as though you got some fans out there' said Ross to him.

"Yes it does" replied Jimmy."

"Can't be bad let's hope they bring me some good luck."

Dill and Ross were discussing the next approach shot to the green.

The flag was on the right hand side back of the green 'watch the, bunkers on the right' he told Ross'.

'I know' answered Ross.

Ross took his shot it bounced off the mound of grass and rolled in to, the bunker.

He banged the golf club on the ground.

'What shot was that' asked Dill.

'I told you to watch the bunkers on the right.

Don't remind me replied Ross annoyed.

They walked up to bunker, assessed the next shot.

At least it's not plugged in the sand and you've got a descent lie, of ball', Dill said to him.

Ross just grunted took his club and hit the ball, it landed on, the green on edge of the hole.

'Good shot, now just tap it in the hole' said Dill.

Ross tapped the ball and it dropped into hole.

'Right on to the next tee' he said to Dill.

Walking off he was annoyed he'd put his ball in the bunker, in the first place.

The next few holes were played with close scores.

Jimmy had had a birdie on the 13th hole so he was happy he would get, a shot back on the score card.

Ross had teed off on the 16th hole sliced it in front of a tree.

He looked at his caddy.

Dill knew what he was thinking he could read his mind sometimes he, would say to Ross.

Over the top of the trees!!

They decided Ross would go for it.

He hit his shot over the top of the trees and it landed on the green.

'Great one' said Dill.

'I knew you could do it.'

'You put all your concentration in to that swing'.

They walked on to the green.

Ross lined up and sunk his putt.

Dill looked at Ross gave him a high five.

When Jimmy was taking his third shot towards the green he plugged, it in the left side bunker,

"Dam and dam" what did I do that for" he asked himself slinging the, club down on the ground.

He was annoyed with himself.

It took him three more shots to finish the hole.

Billy Hopkins was catching Ross up on the scoreboard.

He was only three shots behind.

Jeff Daniels was not doing so well and was 6 over par.

Jimmy looked at the leader board whilst walking down the fairway.

All this technology meant he could keep an eye on the scores on the, course.

'Big mistake' said his caddy.

'Concentrate on your game'.

Jimmy knew he had to keep his cool.

He'd just given the last hole to Ross and wasn't pleased, about it.

The camera man was walking along side the course taking, photographs of the players.

They had all taken their shots on the next hole.

Ross knew he was in a good position on the leader board.

A large group of spectators were following Ross and Jimmy around,
the course.
They wanted to make sure they saw the final putt on the last hole.
 Jimmy still had a group of ladies following him and cheering that,
lifted his spirits.
Then what else would Ross expect of Jimmy.
 Ross would smile to himself thinking that was Jimmy all over.
Jimmy's caddy walked over to him and put his hand on his shoulder.
'Calm down Jimmy' he suggested.
 Jimmy took four putts to get the ball in the hole.
He walked off feeling annoyed threw his putter to Big Joe.
Joe picked it up off the grass and cleaned it before placing it back in,
the bag.
 When they got to the 17th hole Ross thought he'd got it in the bag.
He was leading by two shots.
 He missed a short putt on the green leaving it on the edge of the hole.
 When Ross turned around he saw and heard a young lady shout over,
to him.
 How on earth could you miss a short putt like that? She shouted.
 He stared at the lady in disapproval.
 She stared back at him then gave a false smile.
 Dill waived to her.
 Ross had finished putting out.
He walked over to Dill.
 "Who's that woman over there?"He asked.
Dill replied" that's Charlie Greaves daughter."
"What Charlie who's in the tournament"? Ross asked.
 "Yeah that's right' was Dills reply."

Charlie was in his 50s and was going to retire from the professional, tours after the tournament.

Laura had flown in to see her dad play.

"Well whoever she is" said Ross to Dill.

"I didn't like the remark about my putting".

Who does she think she is shouting her mouth off?"

"Well not everyone likes what people say' commented Dill.

You'll just have to let it go in one ear and out the other forget about it."

'Although, she will be with her dad at the dinner tonight, said Dill.

"Oh will she?" replied Ross.

"I might have a few words with her about it he commented.

'Leave it Ross she's not worth getting up tight over' answered Dill.

Let's get to the next tee.

Jimmy putted out on the last hole.

'Ross took the last hole walked over to Jimmy and shook his hand'.

No hard feelings' he said' just a game Jimmy'.

Let's go check our cards' said Dill,' make sure there's no mistake and, it's all in order. "

They shook hands with the other players and walked off the green.

The President of the club came out to address the crowd.

He went on to say that the presentation would follow in fifteen, minutes.

A table was set out with the trophies 1st and 2nd place winner to be, presented.

They crowd waited for the presentation to begin.

The president, the caption, and the club sponsor came out of the hotel. They lined up on the 18th green to present the trophy to the winner, and runner up of the tournament

Ross stood there in anticipation waiting for the winner to be, announced.

The president walked up to the microphone.

He spoke to the crowd about the players and the sponsors of the, tournament.

'It gives me great pleasure' he said 'to introduce the sponsor of the, tournament to present the trophy to a well deserved winner'. Ross Portland'.

The crowd applauded and cheered.

The sponsor of the tournament lifted the cup from the table to present, to Ross.

Ross walked up towards him to collect the cup.

He congratulated Ross on his win and handed him the cup.

Whilst shaking hands with Ross the sponsor remarked about the, missed putt on 17th.

Ross smiled 'I know I couldn't believe it myself' he said.

He could feel the embarrassment in his face.

He could see Laura in the front row of the crowd out the corner of his, eye.

Ross walked up to the microphone to say a few words thanking, the sponsor and the host also complimented the ground staff for, the condition off the course,

He complimented the other players.

He thanked the crowd for all their support.

Then he held up the cup and kissed it.

The crowd applauded his win Ross stepped aside.

The president then went on to say the runner up of the competition is, Rocki Narn.

Rocki walked up to take his prize said a few words.

Then he stood next to Ross for photographs to be taken of them both, with the sponsor of the tournament.

The local photographer was taking shots of them both holding up their, cups.

These would be shown in the next addition of the paper and golf, magazines.

Jimmy walked up to Ross and shook his hand.

"Well done mate" said Jimmy you deserved it.

Mary, Phillip, and Josie gathered around Ross to congratulate him.

The caddies sorted out the clubs whilst the men went to the bar to, have a well deserved drink.

Then they headed back to their room in the hotel aware they had a, little time for a rest before they made their way to the evening, celebrations.

Jimmy walked in to his room still thinking about his game and the, silly, mistake he had made.

He was annoyed with himself.

Still he only had himself to blame for losing his temper around the, course.

He couldn't blame his caddie big Joe.

All the way round the course Joe kept on saying to him calm down, Jimmy.

Anyway it was all over and Ross had won the tournament.

Maybe next time he thought to himself.

Chapter 7

Jimmy looked at his watch.

He knew he could get in a short nap before showering.

Then there would be an evening meal and dancing.

Not that he was much of a dancer.

He liked to stand and observe the way the women moved their bodies, swaying their hips to the music on the dance floor.

It turned Jimmy on.

All Jimmy had on his mind was if he was going to pull tonight.

Ross was too excited to rest.

All he could do was admire the cup on the table in his room.

He inspected the cup to see if the engraver had spelt his name right.

Then of course he would thought Ross

Ross walked into the bar area in the restaurant and looked around for, Jimmy.

He knew he would be around there somewhere propping up the bar.

"Your round get them in, mines a pint."Ross said to Jimmy.

As he walked up to the bar.

As Jimmy ordered the drinks, he nudged Ross.

"Look at the other end of the bar she's a bit of alright look at the legs, on that" he said to him.

"Stop it "said Ross.

"Have a bit of respect that's Brins wife."

"He wouldn't like to hear you talk about her like that."

"Just looking" was Jimmy's reply.

"That's what you always say, as long as it's just looking and nothing, else on your mind" said Ross.

"What do you take me for' asked Jimmy?

"Don't answer that" was his quick reply.

Ross's mind went back to remember the night,

Jimmy got caught out with Rocki Narn's wife Ella

She's a bit of a floozy Ross would say to Jimmy.

Be careful.

Rocki Narn had been drinking heavily all night.

He was boasting out loud to the lads about his younger days with the, ladies.

Ella felt embarrassed and angry at the same time.

So upset she decided she was going to have an early night.

Jimmy said he was going to his room to get some more cigarettes and, offered to escort her to her room.

When she got to the door she burst into tears,

Jimmy didn't know what to do so he invited her into his room.

"Don't get upset "he told her 'we all know what Rocki's like when he's, had too much to drink'.

Sitting on the edge of the bed she poured her heart out to Jimmy.

How unhappy she was with Rocki's drinking.

She knew they had drifted apart it was a loveless relationship she told, Jimmy.

Jimmy started feeling sorry for her and put his arms around her, hugged her and dried the tears from her eyes.

That's when it all happened.

Jimmy couldn't help himself.

They both fell back onto the bed and started kissing.

Oh Jimmy she moaned.

Jimmy could feel the lust in himself he wanted her so badly.

His hands wandered between her thighs.

She unbuttoned his shirt and her hands were all over his chest.

He helped her to slip out of her dress.

They were both madly undressing each other.

He tore off her bra, tugging at her tights and under pants throwing, them across the floor.

They both lay there naked.

He pulled her naked body towards him.

She could feel the warmth of his skin against hers.

He was sucking on her breast like a baby.

They both felt the passion.

The strength of his sexual needs for her grew he could feel the heat, rising in his body the swelling of his loins.

He couldn't hold back any longer they were making love.

Ella's heavy breathing and gasping for breath.

She couldn't remember the last time Rocki had made her feel like this.

The excitement of being caught made it more daring for them both.

When it was all over they lay there exhausted and laughing.

Like two school children wondering if they would get caught.

At that moment they could hear voices along the corridor.

"OH my god that's Rocki voice" Ella said.

"What do I do now?"Jimmy.

"For a start you can get yourself dressed and tidied up'.

Jimmy told her.

Jimmy quickly gathered up his clothes from the floor and got dressed.

"You wait here Ella' Jimmy said her,' Rocki knows I came up to fetch, some cigarettes."

"Give it five minutes and then slip out the door then get into the lift'.

"When the door closes press the button to open it again then step out, the lift'.

"Let him think you came looking for him' Jimmy told her.

"Ok Jimmy' she replied anxiously.

Jimmy closed the bedroom door behind him.

As he walked down the corridor he brushed by Rocki.

"Hey Jimmy' Rocki said to him Slurring his words.

"Have you seen my wife Ella?"

"No' replied Jimmy."

"I just came up for some cigarettes."

"Bet you did' Rocki replied?"

"What do you mean by that?" asked Jimmy.

"We all know what you're like for the ladies, commented Rocki.

"What's it to you? Jimmy said.

"Anyway you should take more care of your lady."

"Didn't you notice how upset she was earlier this evening, but then, you wouldn't you "Jimmy told him.

"I think you'd better mind your own business said Rocki."

"What are you going to do about it then?" replied Jimmy.

Just then Ella came creeping out of Jimmy's room.

Rocki stood there starring her in the face.

"You dirty little slut."He said to her.

'And as for you Jimmy' he threw a hard punch at Jimmy,

He fell against the wall.

Jimmy retaliated and threw one back.

Ella stood there screaming shouting, stop it, stop it, you two'.

By then other people had heard what was going on and came rushing, up the stairs.

Ross and some of the other players pulled them apart.

Rocki was bleeding profusely from his nose.

He grabbed hold of Ella's arm and pushed her through their bedroom, door.

'Leave me alone you bastard' she screamed.

'Get in there' Rocki replied, 'you're showing yourself up and with him, of all people'.

Rocki slammed the door shut.

Jimmy was nursing a cut lip and cut below his eye, the blood poured, from his nose down his shirt.

By that time the security man had come running up the stairs showing, a gun in his holster.

Ross meet him face to face he apologised and explained that it was all, sorted out.

"Well we don't want any more trouble from you lot.

We also have other guests to think of "demanded the security guard.

"So let there be no more disturbances".

With that the guard walked away looking over his shoulder until Ross, and Jimmy was out of view.

Ross took Jimmy back to his room.

"Don't tell me he sighed, I think I know what that was about."

"Don't ask'? Jimmy told him.

'It's none of my business' said Ross."

"Let's get some ice on that lip' Ross told him.

Jimmy was angry, stop fussing I'll sort it'.

Ross looked Jimmy in the eye' how could you be so bloody stupid', he said to him.

'Of all the people you had to get involved with, tonight of all nights, Rocki Narn's wife.

'I can't understand you sometimes Jimmy'.

Ross closed the door behind him and headed to his room.

Wondering why Jimmy had to get involved any way with the player's, wives.

After all there were plenty of single women about.

That man will never learn.

Chapter 8

The next morning Rocki and Ella left early.

Ross went down to the restaurant to have breakfast.

He walked across where Jimmy was sitting.

He pulled out a chair and sat down next to him.

Jimmy apologized to him for the scene he had caused the night before.

He was nursing a swollen lip.

Ross also saw he had a shiner of a bruise under his right eye.

'You look as though you've been in a boxing ring.

He said to Jimmy.

Don't remind me it sure feels like it, answered Jimmy.

"What was I thinking about '? He said "realizing how stupid he had, been.

"Well let that be a lesson to you Jimmy" replied Ross.

Any way it's in the past.

But then Ross knew Jimmy was his own worst enemy sometimes.

Ross was wondering why that thought had come to mind at that, moment.

Forget it he thought he was determined to enjoy the night ahead.

Some of the player wives and girlfriends were already on the dance, floor.

As Ross leaned on the bar a hand tapped him on his shoulder.

"Hello you" the voice said,"

Fancy seeing you all dressed up in your dickey bow."

Ross turned around he already knew by the sound of her voice who it, was, Charlie Greaves daughter,

I'm Laura, she introduced herself,

"I know who you are" said Ross.

'Really?' said Laura.

"You're the one, who commented about me missing my putt."

"Well surely you're not going to take offence at a little remark like, that'? She told him.

"Tell you what I'll buy you a drink if it makes you feel better about, it."? Laura offered.

"You don't have to do that?'

"After all I really shouldn't have missed."

"Let me buy you one' asked Ross.

"Oh so we're friends now. "smiled Laura.

"Well how can a girl refuse?"

"OK I'll have a glass of wine."She replied.

'Red or White' answered Ross.

'White please' was her reply.

'Large or small' he said smiling.

Laura was beginning to wonder if he was taking the mickey.

'As you are offering I'll have a large one please', Replied Laura.

Ross decided to order a bottle of white wine.

'Are you trying to get me drunk' she said to him.

'No it saves me coming back' he said smiling.

Laura looked lovely in her tight dress and high heels.

It showed of her slim elegant figure.

Ross admired her long legs.

Ross paid the barman for the drinks.

"Let's go and sit with the family "Ross suggested.

He collected the drinks from the bar.

They walked across the room to the table.

"Hello you two" said Phillip, have you come to join us"?

Phillip rose from his seat to pull out a chair for Laura.

"Thank you "she said and sat next to him.

Ross place the drinks on the table then sat next to Laura.

Jimmy winked at Ross as though to say you're in there boy.

Jimmy was busy chatting to Josie at the bar.

"What are you drinking" he asked her.

"Well if you're buying I'll have champagne' she replied.

"Cheeky now you've got expensive taste' he said.

"Ok I'll settle for a G&T then."

"Not quite the same but thank you "She replied.

Jimmy ordered Josie's a drink and carried it over to the table where, they all sat.

He put the drinks down on the table then proceeded to pull out a chair, for Josie.

"Now don't say I don't know how to treat a lady."

He told her.

'Hee' Josie laughed, "Ok you win "she replied.

They all sat together chatting around the table.

Ross had introduced Laura to his mum and dad.

Laura turned around and caught the sight of her dad at the bar.

She got up and went over to him.

"Dad, come and join us at Ross's table'.

"Ok I'll be there in a minute love' He told her.

Charlie walked over to the table where Laura was sitting with, Ross family, carrying a pint in his hand.

Ross pulled out a chair so Charlie could sit next to Laura.

Charlie thanked Ross then congratulated him on his win today.

Ross introduced his family to Charlie saying, this is my mum Mary, and dad Phillip and of course Josie my sister.

Charlie shook hands with them.

'Pleased to meet you all' he said.

"Don't forget Jimmy" Josie remarked.

"We all know Jimmy" was Ross's reply.

'So what do you think of your son a proud day for you I'm sure.

"Charlie asked then went on to say.

"It was a well deserved win'.

"All though it was a close game' he remarked.

"Yes' answered Mary 'we're very proud of him.

'Phillip loves to come to the tournaments to see Ross play when he, can'.

Phillip used to play himself a few years ago, but stopped for while, when he had his heart attack'.

What with the car sales business to run, it keeps him busy.

He does try to get in the odd game now and then.

Sometime Ross will take him for a game when he's at home between, tournaments.

Phillip talked through the night with Charlie about the car sales side,
of the business.

Charlie was getting on well with him.

As the night went on they sat talking and listening to the band playing.
Ross was getting to like Laura.

She not only had a good figure she was clever, witty and had a lovely,
smile and gorgeous brown eyes.

Laura's feet were tapping to the rhythm of the music.

"Would you like to dance Ross? Asked Laura"

"Well I might have two left feet" He replied.

"Oh come on" she urged him.

'Alright but I have warned you' answered Ross.

'Don't blame me if I step on your toes'.

With that they were heading for the dance floor.

Jimmy and Josie were laughing at themselves trying to jive.

The music was fast and they were a bit out of turn with their steps.
But they were enjoying themselves.

After a couple of lively dances the DJ put on some slow music.
Jimmy looked at Josie".

'Shall we sit this one out? He asked.

'Fine by me' she relied' I'm wacked."

With that they both walked off the dance floor.

'Think we both deserve a drink after all that jiving' Josie' said to
Jimmy.

Ross wasn't one for smooch dancing.

But he liked the feel of having Laura in his arms.

They moved closer to each other.

Ross put his arms around her and held her tightly.

He smelt the aroma of her perfume.

It was Intoxicating.

Laura quite liked the feel of his strong arms around her.

They felt muscular too.

"You ok Ross'? She asked."

Ross replied" it's a long time since I danced with a woman.

'I'm not much of a dancer,
Jimmy and I prefer to enjoy a drink'
"I know dad mentioned that's why you were late this morning'.
"Oh did he now?" smirked Ross.
She smiled at him and they both laughed out loud.
The night went by too quickly.
Josie spent the rest of the evening talking to Jimmy.
She never realized he was so much fun.
When the evening came to an end they all said their goodnights and,
were off to bed.
Ross went to bed wondering what time Laura would turn up for,
breakfast.

Ross walked in to the dining area the next morning looking a bit blurry,
eyed.
The players were all discussing yesterday's game.
Also what tournament they would be playing next.
Laura entered the room followed by her dad and sat down,
near the window.
She looked across at Ross and smiled.
Ross waited till they had finished their breakfast then walked over to,
Laura.
Asking her what she was up to that day.
"Oh I'll just hang around with dad for a while, before I head back,
home" she told him.
"I'm a working girl you know."
Charlie joined in the conversation, 'never know when you'll need a,
solicitor It's good to have one in the family."
"Yes said Jimmy" joining in on the next table.
"But don't they know how to charge cost me a fortune for my divorce. "

When they got up to leave Ross caught Laura by the arm.

"It would be nice if I could see you again I enjoyed our evening ",
He told her.

"Yes so did I' she replied.
"I'll give you my number if you like'.

"In fact I'll text you it if you give me yours."
With that they exchanged numbers.

"I'm busy next week I'm working on a big case.

"I only managed to get to this tournament because dad was playing."
"I wanted to have some time with him."
"That's fine with me said Ross' you take care and have a safe journey,"
"You to" Laura replied.

Ross shook hands with Charlie.
"Nice to spend some time with you Charlie let's hope we see each,
other again."
"Let's hope so too, you take care' Remarked, Charlie.

"Well "said Jimmy "what are you up to?'
It's not like you to ask for a ladies number."
"I reckon you got the love bug."

"Don't be daft Jimmy' retorted Ross 'I only asked her for her,
number."

"She might change her mind when she's back home."

"Doesn't look like it to me she seemed quite taken up with you on,
the dance floor" Replied Jimmy.
"We'll see won't we' said Ross.

Chapter 9

Unbeknown to Ross, Jimmy had asked Josie for her number and if, she liked ten pin bowling.

'It's a long time since I've played she said.

He liked her independence and determination to succeed in business. Running the florist and being there for her parents.

They had agreed to meet up with some friends the next Saturday night, when Jimmy and Ross returned home.

The bowling alley sounded good fun.

Jimmy didn't want to say too much to Ross.

He had taken a liking to Josie.

Josie knew Ross may not approve because of Jimmy track record with, the ladies.

Josie had been in contact with Laura, to ask her to join her and the girls, on the Saturday night.

Laura was bringing her friend Maggie along.

Maggie had been a champion ten pin Bowler.

They were sworn to secrecy not to let on to the men.

Jimmy phoned Josie after arriving home from the tournament.

"Well young lady have you arranged the bowling for Saturday night?" He asked.

"Of course girls against the boys she replied'.

'Really'? Jimmy said laughing.

"You heard" she said to him.

"You're on we'll thrash you "Jimmy told her'

"Oh yeah we'll wait and see shall we?" came Josie's Reply.

We'll all meet at the bowling alley at 8'oclock."
"Don't be late "said Josie.
See you then' 'replied Jimmy.
Can't wait?' he said, as he rubbed his hands together.
There in for a right thrashing he thought to himself.
It soon came around to Saturday night.
Ross and Jimmy turned up at the bowling alley with their friends.
Josie didn't let on to Ross that Laura and her friend Maggie was,
coming along too.
Ross was surprised to see Laura there.
But he was delighted at the same time.
"Fancy seeing you here how come?' He asked her.
"Josie invited us, you ok with that Ross, She replied.
"More than ok its lovely to see you."He answered.
'By the way this is my friend Maggie' she said introducing her to Ross.
'Pleased to meet you Maggie' replied Ross.
As Maggie shook Ross's hand she made a comment.
"You won't say that if we beat you'
"Oh competition time is it, said Ross smiling at her.
"Just you wait and see "
"You girls might be buying the drinks tonight" Ross said laughing.
"Did you hear that girls."Shouts Josie.
"It maybe the other way round."
Right lads tactic time." mentioned Ross.
Jose laughed, looking at them.
Team talk is it then let's gets our heads together girls.
"She told them.
They all had a great night out, the girls beat the boys.
Josie didn't tell Jimmy that two of the girls were bowling champs.
They would never live it down if they didn't have a return match.
"We'll see what you're made of on our return match said Jimmy."
"Return match can you hear that girls."
"Wow their glutten for punishment "Laughed Josie.
"Right you're on what do you say Laura."

"Sounds as though they don't like to be beaten by the women',
replied Laura.

Ross couldn't believe what he was hearing.

Ross Laughed out loud.

"Return match then lads what do you say."

"Are you sure you girls know what you're doing." he told them.

"Cheeky beggars" said Josie to her friends.

"We've just thrashed them and their coming back for more."

Let the fun begin" said Josie winking at Laura.

Chapter 10

Ross and Jimmy knew they had a few days to relax at home before; they would be on their way to their next tournament in America.
The flight times were sorted.
Tee times were booked ahead of schedule.
It gave Ross time to relax a little and chill out with the family.
Also Ross could get some drinking time in with Jimmy.
Ross reminisced, it only seemed like yesterday.
When Jimmy walked into the car show room Ross's Dad owned.
Jimmy was looking for a sports car and had his eye on one on display, on the forecourt.
He knew Ross took pride in his sports car.
Jimmy wanted to go one better he wanted a flashy type.
They had done a deal that day so Ross took him for a drink to, celebrate.
They remained good friends and started playing golf together.
Little did Ross know that it would be the start of Jimmy's competitiveness between them two?
Ross picked up the Sunday paper trying to concentrate on reading it.
His mind went back to Laura and what a good time they all had last, night.
He reached across for his mobile phone that lay on the coffee table.
Picked it up then proceeded to scroll down his list of contacts for, Laura's number.
He hesitated a second before calling her.
Afraid she may not answer.

The mobile rang a few times before Laura answered.

"Hi it's me Ross' he said.

"I thought I'd give you a call."

'You didn't mind did you.' asked Ross.

'No not at all 'replied Laura.

"I was thinking of you also said Laura 'and what a good night we all, had."

'Yes I think we all had a good time' replied Ross.

They talked for a while.

Ross went on to tell her his next tournament was in America.

"Would you like to go out for a meal when I return home?" he asked, her.

"Yes I'd like that very much" replied Laura.

"I'll give you a call then when I return' said Ross.

"I'll look forward to it have a safe flight' replied Laura.

They both said their goodbyes.

Laura was hoping Ross would keep to his word when he returned, home.

All Ross could think about between his games was Laura.

On the return flight home, as soon as the plane landed at the airport, immediately after Ross had collected his luggage he phoned Laura.

He was anxious to hear her voice.

Laura was also pleased to hear his voice.

He asked if she would like to go out with him for a meal on Saturday, night.

That would be very nice she said to him,

I'll pick you up at Seven o'clock he told her.

I'll look forward to it came her reply.

When Saturday arrived Ross turned up on time to pick up Laura.

There's a nice little Italian restaurant in town recently opened.

I thought you'd like to try it if that's ok with you' he asked her.

"I've booked a table for us just in case".

"But if you prefer somewhere else I can cancel' asked Ross.

"No that's sounds lovely, I love Italian food' replied Laura.
"That's ok then we'll see what it's like." Ross said.
The place was busy and Italian music was playing in the background.
The décor and atmosphere of the restaurant made you almost feel you, were in Italy itself.

As the waiter showed them to their table, Laura spotted her boss, sitting at a table across the room.
"Hi Laura what are you doing here?" he shouted to her.
Laura just smiled.
Ross looked up from the menu.
"Looks like I have some competition. "He commented.
"Don't be silly he's my boss he's with his wife she's just come out the, ladies cloak room" smiled Laura.
"That's alright" said Ross he felt more at ease.

The night passed by quickly, the conversation had flowed they both, felt relaxed in each other's company.
The food was enjoyable, with delicious Italian dishes.
The wine complemented the meal.
Towards the end of the evening Ross waved the waiter over.
"May I have the bill please?" he asked.
"Yes sir" came the reply 'was everything to your satisfaction'? asked, the waiter.
Before Ross could answer Laura said to the waiter.
"Complements to the chef, the food was superb we'll be back.
We will be recommending the restaurant to our friends'.
Ross looked at her "looks like I'll be seeing you again then."
"Don't see why not, if that's ok with you?'
'Of course' Ross replied.
Ross helped Laura put on her Coat then they headed to the car.
On the way home they talked about their families.

Ross turned in to Laura's drive she lived in a nice two bedroom house.

Laura looked at Ross "would you like to come in for a drink"? She asked.

"Well if it's not too late for you' said Ross.

With that they both got out of the car.

Laura opened the front door.

Ross followed her into the lounge.

'Take a seat' she said to him,' tell me what you'd like to drink'.

"I think I'll just have a coffee if you don't mind "answered Ross.

"Sure' asked Laura.

Have to think about drinking' Ross said to her.

Whilst Laura was busy making the coffee, Ross looked at the photos, around the room of Charlie on various golf courses.

"Looks like your dad has won some trophies in his time" he said to, her.

"Yes" replied Laura.

'Mum used to love to see him play."

Laura had told Ross about her mum passing away five years ago.

'Good thing dad had his golf to keep him going.'

'Otherwise I don't know how he would have managed' said Laura.

Laura arrived with the coffee placed it on the table in front of them, then sat down next to Ross.

"I've really enjoyed this evening "commented Ross.

"So have I' replied Laura.

They sat close together.

Ross leaned over and kissed her.

She blushed then felt a tingling through her body.

Ross didn't want to out stay his welcome and spoil things.

He had grown very fond of Laura in such a short time.

'I think I'd better go' he said 'it's getting late'.

I've got a few days before I'm off to the next tournament.

"Can I see you again Laura when I get back he asked. "Maybe I could, phone you whilst I'm away if that's alright with you."

"That would be nice" she said.

With that they kissed good night and Ross went on his way.

Talking to Ross about her mum, made Laura think about the times her, mum was alone.

Her dad was away a lot from one place to the other with his golfing.

But that was his life his golf she understood that.

He would always phone her when he arrived at his new destination.

Sometimes she would try to get to a tournament to see him play.

She had her life also and wanted Charlie to enjoy his.

"I'll phone you when I get to the Hotel' He would say to her.

How those words now sounded familiar to Laura.

Ross couldn't believe how he felt about Laura.

Was he in love, he felt butterfly's in his stomach at the mention, of her name.

Laura knew also she'd grown to like Ross in such a short time.

Jimmy wanted to show off his new car so arranged to pick up Ross.

Jimmy packed his case loaded up the car and was on his way.

He pulled off the main road and headed down the narrow lane.

He admired the big posh houses as he drove by.

Ross's house stood back from off the road and had a stunning tree, lined driveway.

Jimmy pulled into the edge of the drive.

As he got out the car he knew why Ross had chosen to live here.

It felt peaceful no one to disturb you apart from a few houses along, the road.

Must be some money people living down this area he thought to, himself.

Jimmy pressed the button on the intercom.

'It's me Ross' he said.

'I know 'answered Ross.

'How did you know' commented Jimmy.

'From the bloody camera' came the reply.

Ross pressed the button that opened the big iron gates.

Jimmy pulled up to the front door.

'Be with you in a minute Jimmy' said Ross.

I've just finished packing my case.

"Did you have a late night out with Charlie's daughter?"Jimmy asked.

''It's not like you not to be ready on time it must have been good, night."

Ross ignored Jimmy's remark.

He knew what Jimmy was hinting at, quickly replied to his smutty, comments, 'not the way you're thinking Jimmy'.

"She a very nice girl, Charlie would like her to be treated, respectively."

"Yes she is very nice, pretty as well and educated."

'Ok I didn't mean to offend her' replied Jimmy.

"Anyway' said Ross 'we've got a flight to catch."

They were soon on their way to the airport.

What Jimmy didn't want to let on to Ross was that he had taken a, shine to Josie?

Josie and Jimmy had also been out for a drink that weekend.

They had so much fun on their return night out bowling.

The boy's had beaten the girl's.

So they had arranged a return match to decide the winners.

Josie had realized, what with the shop and visiting her parents.

It had left little time for her to have some fun.

There had been many Saturday nights out with the girls.

Not that she didn't like going out with them.

But now she thought something was missing in her life.

Was that something Jimmy?

Chapter 11

This can't be right? Josie thought to herself.

Her mind was on Jimmy all the time.

Ross always warned her about his womanizing.

Had she seen a different side to him that no one else had?

Underneath he was fun to be with.

They had similar tastes.

Maybe they were both good for each other.

They wanted their relationship to be discreet for the time being.

She was beginning to have feelings for Jimmy.

Something she never thought would happen.

When she went home at night she felt a little lonely without his, company.

He may be Jack the lad in Ross's eyes.

In Josie's eye's she saw the caring side of Jimmy.

She was content when she was in his company.

Ross may not approve of Jimmy seeing his sister.

He knew Jimmy was a love them and leave them type.

Then on to the next catch.

He always used to say to Josie, 'don't end up with someone like him'.

'He's a good friend but lousy with the women'.

But it was her life not Ross's.

The weeks passed by.

Josie and Jimmy saw each other when Jimmy got back off his tours.

They kept it quiet to themselves.

Jimmy knew if Ross found out he was seeing Josie,

He would have him breathing down his neck.

Wondering what he was up to with his sister.

He could hear him saying.

"Don't get too attached' she's my sister."

But then after all, Josie was a grown woman it was none of Ross's business.

Why were they so concerned about him?

Josie only saw Ross when he came home from tournaments.

Ross and Laura kept in touch and saw each other when they could.

Things were getting serious between the two of them.

Ross knew Laura was the girl for him.

He booked a table at the Italian restaurant they had been to on their first night out.

He had particularly asked to be seated at the same table.

He arranged to pick up Laura at 7-30 in the evening.

When he arrived at her house he walked in with a big bouquet of flowers.

'What are these for'? Laura asked.

'Do I need to have an excuse to bring you flowers'? Commented Ross.

'No' replied Laura.

'Their beautiful bet I know where they came from'.

'Never you mind' answered Ross.

Laura gave him a kiss.

'I'll just put them in water' she said to him 'then we'll be on our way'.

Laura had no Idea Ross was going to propose to her that night.

On entering the restaurant Ross gave his name to the manager,
explaining to him, that he previous had booked a particular table for an, evening meal.

The manager checked the list.

'Oh yes' Mr. Portland he replied if you would like to follow me.

He escorted Ross and Laura to their table.

He pulled out the chair from under the table, requesting Laura to take a, seat

May I take your coat' he asked her.

'Yes please' she replied

Laura handed him her coat.

The manager went on to explain the waiter would be with them shortly.

'This is nice' said Laura to Ross' it's the same table we sat at on our, first date.

Ross pretended to ignore her comment.

 The waiter sorted out the drinks and took their orders for starters and, main courses.

When they had finished their main course, on clearing the table the, waiter asked if they would like see the dessert menu.

'Yes please' they both replied and chose their desserts.

 Ross got up from the table and went to the bar to order a bottle of, champagne.

Laura wondered what he was up to.

'What are you up to' she asked Ross as he sat back down at the table, 'Nothing' he replied.

Just then the champagne arrived.

'Champagne I didn't order champagne' said Laura.

 'No but I did' replied Ross

Ross was getting nervous.

What if she say's no?

 He had not thought of that.

'Their taking their time bringing the desserts' said Ross.

'They will be here in a minute 'replied Laura.

'Anyway what's the rush'?

Just then the waiter came over with the desserts.

Coffee panacotta with hazelnuts he said.

Oh that's mine replied Laura.

Limón cello semifreddo with strawberries he said looking at Ross.

'Yes' 'thank you' replied Ross to him.

The waiter placed each of their desserts in front of them.

'Oh that looks nice Laura said to Ross looking at his dessert with the, big fresh strawberries.

 'Maybe I should have ordered that instead.

'You can swap if you like' said Ross.

 'No it's alright I like coffee panacotta.

The waiter turned to Ross 'would you like me to open the champagne, for you' he asked.

'That would be very nice' Ross replied.

The waiter popped the cork then poured the champagne.

Ross thanked him.

Laura was getting more suspicious

'Is there something you need to tell me she said to Ross?

'Yes there is' he nervously replied'

'Laura we have known each other for some time now'.

'Thiers no one I love more than you'.

Laura blushed.

Ross pulled a box out of his jacket pocket.

He opened the lid in front of Laura.

'What I'm trying to say is, will you marry me'?

Laura stared at the ring a beautiful single diamond.

He waited for Laura to answer.

'Don't keep me in suspense' he said to her.

'Yes Yes I will. 'She replied.

Ross took the ring from the box and placed it on Laura's finger.

The people in the restaurant cheered and clapped congratulating, them both.

Laura had tears in her eyes.

So this is what the champagne was all about.

'Just one thing' she said, what now thought Ross.

'How did you know this was the one I liked' asked Laura.

'Well you know when we went in to the jewelers the other week to, fetch my watch, and you were trying on the rings you kept admiring, that one, I could see it in your eyes'

'Also it fitted perfectly'.

'I went back the next day to buy it' said Ross.

'Well it's beautiful Ross' she told him, then she kissed him.

When it came to pay the bill the manager said the champagne was on, the house.

Ross thanked him.

Then they made their way home.

The next day Laura decided to phone her dad.

"How are you dad? She asked him'

"I'm ok 'replied Charlie 'It's lovely to hear your voice.

'What have you been up to then?"

"Well you know that Ross and I have been together a while now."

"He's asked me to marry him and I've said yes"

Charlie was quiet for a minute at the other end of the phone.

"If he's the one for you then I am very happy, he's a nice man Laura', "he replied.

"But you know what it's like with him being on tour all the time', said Charlie.

'As long as you're happy then it's up to you two."

'It was hard for your mum and me being away from each other some, of the time."

'She was a good woman to put up with it'.

'But you're a grown women and I'm sure you'll work it out between, you' remarked her dad.

'Thanks dad I'm coming to see you at the weekend and we can catch, up' she replied.

You take care love you" he said.

Laura put the phone down and thought about what she was going to, wear.

She was going to have a meal at Ross's parents.

Ross and Jimmy had gone for a drink after their game.

Best hole the 19th Jimmy would say.

Ross looked at Jimmy.

"I want to ask you something' said Ross.

Jimmy wondered what he was going to say.

Did Ross know Jimmy was seeing Josie on the quiet?

He knew she would be mad if he let on about it.

"Only say yes if you really want too' said Ross.

"What's that' replied Jimmy cautiously.

"God you look so serious Ross you're spooking me out. "

"Will you be my best man' Ross asked him.

"You mean you've ask Laura to marry you?"

"It would seem like it else I wouldn't be asking you to be,
My best man"

"Of course I will I'd be honored" Jimmy replied

"That's settled it then he said to Ross let's have a drink to,
you both.

Jimmy sighed thank god it's only that he thought to himself.

Then he ordered another round of drinks.

Chapter 12

Laura got on well with Ross's parents.

They were looking forward to having her as a daughter in law.

They would be getting married at the local church.

They had arranged to have their wedding reception at the Victoria, Hotel which was two miles out of town.

It was renowned for a romantic wedding venue.

Laura, Ross, and the family went to several wedding exhibitions.

Josie was excited Laura had asked her to be chief bridesmaid and, asked her to arrange the flowers for the wedding.

The other bridesmaids were Maggie and another of Laura's friend.

There were fun days out shopping together trying on dresses and shoes.

Ross would say once he had chosen the suits for the men he could, leave the rest to the women.

Phillip took care of arranging the car a Rolls Royce.

Laura sorted the photographer.

She got mesmerized when it came to choosing the design of the, wedding cake but kept it simple.

Josie also had the pleasure of arranging the hen party.

She had booked a fun weekend away for the girls.

Laura made sure Ross's mum came with her for the Wedding dress, fittings.

She knew how much her mum would have loved to have been there, to see her trying on the dress.

Some days it brought tears to her eyes.

Knowing her mum would not see her walk down the aisle with her, dad.

The heartache of missing her on her wedding day could not be, measured.

She was having a special bouquet of flowers arranged to put on her, mother's grave on the day.

Ross had discussed with Laura about selling her house and investing, her money.

She loved the area where Ross lived.

She didn't want the hassle of renting out her property.

The up keep of everything.

It would not take too long for her to travel to the office.

It was beautiful big house.

It had security inside and out with electric gates.

Ross had his own gym attached to the house.

A nice tree lined drive with a large garden at the back of the house.

She loved the way the garden shaped into little hiding places.

It would be a great place for children to play hide and seek.

It had a large patio area were they enjoyed sitting out for a meal, or relaxing admiring the garden.

There were several containers of flowers placed artistically around the, patio that brought some colour to the garden.

The sun caught the back of the house late evening time.

They loved nothing more than relaxing outside that time of day with a, glass of wine.

The months went by the invitation had been sent out.

Finally the day had arrived for the wedding.

The men looked very smart in their dark blue suits and top hats.

Laura had chosen a pink carnation for them to wear in their button, hole.

That was her mum's favorite flower.

She wanted her dad to cherish the memories of her on their daughter's, wedding day.

Jimmy was rehearsing his Speech.

"Keep it clean" shouts Ross" don't reveal too many secrets"

"As if I would like the night you got so drunk that you fell in the, bushes with your pants down."

"Now I am wondering what you going to say."

Said Ross concerned.

"Oh don't worry it'll be fine"

"I'll try not to embarrass you too much' Jimmy said.

"Have you got the rings?"Asked Ross.

"In my pocket' answered Jimmy.

"I told you stop worrying. "He laughed.

Laura got up early that morning to take the flowers to her mother's, grave.

She stood there explaining what her dress and the bridesmaid dresses, were like.

Wishing her mum could have been there for her wedding day.

'Dad will look dapper in his Top hat and tails.

Mary and I went with the men when they tried their suits on.

'You should have seen him trying the top hat on.'

'You may like to try the next size up sir said the tailor at the shop to, him.

He looked across at me at that moment, don't say another word young, lady' he said.

We couldn't stop laughing.

'Miss you mum so much' said Laura.

She laid the flowers down and left with a mixture of happiness and, sadness.

The house was buzzing with excitement.
 The bridesmaids were ready.
Josie assisted Laura with her dress.
She looked stunning.
Josie had done a splendid job arranging the bouquet of flowers.
The wedding car's had arrived.
 Charlie was pacing up and down the drive.
 The chauffeur walked up to him.
 "Nervous? he said, yes "replied Charlie "well have a tot of whisky to;
steady your nerves the chauffeur suggested.
He took the flask of whisky from driver's side door and handed it to,
Charlie.
Charlie poured some whisky in the little cup' thanks' he said.
'You're well prepared'; 'something I learned from this job comes in,
handy for the father of the bride."
Charlie went inside the house to see if Laura was ready.
The bridesmaids were on their way to the church, now there was only,
Charlie and Laura left alone.
When he walked into the hall he saw Laura at the top of the stairs,
his eyes were filled with tears" you look lovely' he said.
"If only your mother could have been here to see this day".
"Don't dad" said Laura 'now my mascara will run".
 "I know I've thought about that many times', "I told her all about this,
when I put the flowers on her grave" explained Laura.
Laura brushed away a tear walked down the stairs and hugged her dad;
she felt a mixture of excitement and butterfly's in her stomach.
"Let's go dad she said' I've got a man waiting at the church for me."
The men arrived at the church half an hour before the bride was due to,
arrive friends were gathering.
Ross was fidgeting about, his mum and dad had arrived.
"You look lovely mum' Commented Ross.
"Well I am the mother of the groom so I've got to look special for,
today'.
Your dads just talking to some of the other guest you know,
what he's like," he can't resist talking cars.

"Are you nervous Ross?' His mum asked.
"I've never been so scared I've forgotten my lines.
"Don't worry you'll be alright' she replied.
The vicar nodded to them to take their places as the bride's car had,
arrived.
Charlie looked at her before they stepped out the car.
'You look beautiful he said to her' smiling 'thanks for everything dad',
she said whilst squeezing his hand.
Charlie leaned over and gave her a peck on the cheek.
"Careful dad you'll smudge my makeup' she said laughing.

The photographer was taking photos of the bridesmaids.
The chauffer opened the car door and Charlie got out and helped Laura,
with her dress Josie went to her aide.'
I'll get the flowers 'said Josie.
As Laura walked down the aisle the guest turned to look at her.
Charlie felt a proud father.
The guests were taking in how stunning she looked in her dress.
She stood next to Ross; he turned to her and whispered" you look,
beautiful"
When the vicar asked" who give's this woman?"
Charlie stepped forward and said' I do'.
He felt a slight sadness for a second.
As if he had a hole in his heart.
He quickly reminded himself that he was gaining a good son in law.
The couple said their wedding vows.
Then came the moment when the vicar said 'now you may kiss the,
bride.
They signed the wedding register.
Then the bells rang out and everyone watched as Ross and Laura,
walked down the aisle.
The guest followed the couple outside, gathering for the photographs.
Then they were on their way to the hotel for the reception.

When the other guest arrived at the hotel there were more photographs,
to be taken in the garden by the lake.

 Everyone commented it was the perfect place with the display of',
cascading fountain in the lake.

 Beside the edges of the lake beautiful big flowing willow trees grew,
 it was the most romantic setting for the bride and groom.

The meals were served and the drinks were flowing.

Then there where the speeches were to be made.

 Charlie stood up and said a few words.

He welcomed Ross into his family, and mentioned those who could not,
be with them to celebrate this day.

 Next it was Jimmy's turn.

 Ross sat there wondering what Jimmy was going to say about his best,
friend.

He waited in anticipation, waiting to hear about their nights out on the,
town.

 He had the guest's in stitches, and fortunately it wasn't too bad for,
Ross, although Jimmy kept a few stories to himself.

He knew how far to go with Ross and not embarrass him too much.

 At the end of his speech Jimmy raised his glass of champagne to toast,
the couple.

 The guest's all joined in to wish them both a happy life together.

 Photographs had been taken of the bride and groom cutting the cake.

 The couple enjoyed their evening celebrating their new life together,
with lots of dancing.

 The time came for the Bride and Groom to leave for their honeymoon.

'Don't forget to throw the bouquet' said Laura's friend.

 'Ok are all you girls ready' who's going to be the next bride?'
Laura asked.

 They lined up as Laura got ready.

1-2-3. "Here we go," and up in the air the flowers went the single girls,
all rushed to catch it.

 The surprise looks on Josie's face as she caught the bouquet.

Laura laughed and winked at her.

 "See you when we get back" she shouted.

 Charlie gave her a hug.

"You look after my girl' he instructed to Ross.
"I will don't you worry about that' Replied Ross.
   His parents said their goodbye's and the couple were on their way to, their honeymoon in the Bahamas.
   The remaining guests stayed at the reception the party carried on until, the early hours of the next morning.

Chapter 13

The plane landed on the runway in the Bahamas.

The taxi was waiting to take the newly married couple to their hotel.

They signed in at the reception desk.

'Honeymoon suite' commented the porter, Laura blushed.

Their suitcases were taken to their room and Ross tipped the porter.

Ross took Laura in his arms.

"Well Mrs. Portland is this to your taste?"

Laura's eyes glanced around the room.

"Very nice' she agreed noticing the champagne and chocolates.

"Well we can order an evening meal to be brought up to our room if, you would like that, Ross asked her.

"Ok' agreed Laura 'then we can relax and enjoy the view of the beach, from our balcony."

"Well I might have other things on my mind' commented Ross."

"Remind me what that would be?" smiled Laura.

With that he playfully pushed Laura onto the bed and kissed her neck, caressing her.

His hand wandered down to her thighs.

She could feel his body, the warm of his breath.

Ross kissed her he wanted to take his time.

They had two weeks holiday.

He wanted her to remember the honeymoon and their precious time, together.

He moved from the bed.

"Let's order a meal and sit outside to see the sunset with a glass of, champagne "Suggested Ross.

"Sound likes a good idea to me, whilst you're ordering the meal I'll, take a shower."

Their meal had arrived and Laura was enjoying the evening air and, champagne,

'Ross looked at Laura you look beautiful' he told her' then picked her, up in his arms and carried her over to the bed.

She put her arms around him, holding him tightly she wanted him to, take her.

Slowly he caressed her body she felt the excitement of the passion and, lust.

Ross knew how to make a women feel special.

His tender and slowly love making.

When it was all over they lay there holding each other's naked body.

The warmth of his skin made Laura feel content.

Their days were spent walking along the beach enjoying the sights.

In the evening they watched the sunset and enjoyed the moonlight, nights, while drinking champagne and making love.

Two weeks went by so quickly and the time had arrived for them to, return home.

The flight schedule departure was on time.

As the plane was taking off Laura commented to Ross what a, wonderful time she had.

'So have I' replied Ross and leaned over and kissed her.

Ross picked up his car at the airport after the flight.

'Here give me those cases and you hop into the car'.

'It's back to reality' he told Laura.

'Don't remind me its back to work next week" said Laura.

'Yes and I've got to get back to some practice before the next game', Replied Ross.

Ross pulled up in the drive and jumped out the car,
Rushing to open the front door.
"Wait a minute 'he told Laura.
" What on earth are you up to?' Laura asked.
"Well it's a tradition to carry the bride over the threshold" laughed, Ross.
"You're joking Ross "asked Laura.
"No come here' he said to her.
He lifted Laura into his arms, he felt a lucky man as he carried her, through the door.
Laura couldn't stop laughing.
"Well at least you didn't drop me." She smiled.
"Would I dare?' said Ross smiling.
"It's all those days in the gym building up my muscles" He boasted.
"Well you'd better use them then the cases need getting from the, car." commented Laura.
Charlie had organized some food to be delivered.

'Coffee first' Laura said after the long haul flight she needed a pick, me up caffeine.
Laura was busy in the kitchen.
While Ross put the suit cases in the spare room.
"Lunch is ready" she shouted.
"Ok I'm coming" replied Ross.
After lunch they unpacked the cases, and then they relaxed in the sun, lounge.
"What's your schedule like for the next few weeks?"
Laura asked him.
"Oh we've got the masters coming up,'
So I have to get back to the practice area on Monday'.
I'll phone Jimmy to catch up with him'.
"What about you' he asked Laura.
"Well I can't talk about the case we're on its confidential and it's going, to court next week."
"So you'll have to get used to that side of my job."
'I understand' he replied.

Laura and Ross settled down for the night.
 Phone calls had been made to both families.
   Monday morning came too quickly for both of them.
 Ross was packed and ready to leave.
  "Have a good flight said Laura
 "I Love you and will miss you."She told him.
 'I Love you too' he replied.
 "I'll phone you when we reach the hotel'.
  Looking at her watch" is that the time she said.
 I'd better get going."
   Laura Jumped in her car and was on her way to work.
 She gave Ross a wave as she drove out the driveway.
  Ross had arranged for Jimmy to pick him up.
  They would be on their way to the next event.
 The week went by quickly for Ross.

 No sooner was he home then, he was on to the next tournament.
  Ross had won the masters and was playing in America.
  He was due to fly home early in the morning.
   Laura had sounded mysterious on the phone the evening before.
  He wondered what she was going to say to him.
  Hoping it wasn't going to be about him being away so much.

   When she arrived home from work Ross stood in the kitchen with a,
 serious look on his face.
   "What's the matter Laura you sounded mysterious on the phone'?
 He asked.
 "Is it something I've done or not done? He asked anxiously.
  "Sit down Ross' in fact you might need to get yourself a drink first I,
 have something important to tell you'.
 'No I don't need a drink' he answered.
  He stood there with his arms folded.
  Waiting in anticipation to what Laura had to say.

He could feel the tension in his body.

His chest was rising with his heavy breathing.

The mystery deepened, Ross looked worried

What was it she was going to say to him?

He was bracing himself for what was to come she seemed to be, taking her time thought Ross, why don't she just spit it out.

Laura made a coffee for them both.

Have I got your full attention then? She asked.

His face drained wondering what was coming next.

Sit down and don't look so worried she said to him,

You look as though you've seen a ghost.

That was easy for her to say he thought to himself.

Ross pulled out the chair and sat at the table he reached for his coffee.

I went to see the doctor whilst you were away.

Ross looked shocked "what's the matter?"

"You didn't say anything when I phoned you,

'Are you alright' he asked concerned.

"Yes' she laughed 'of course I am' she answered.

Well what is it then Ross said.

How you would feel about being a father?"

"What you're not, he asked".

'Yes I am came her reply.

Ross was so excited.

"Does anyone else know?"He asked

"No I wanted my husband to be the first."

""How many weeks are you?"Ross asked.

Well the doctor said I'm six weeks so early days yet"

Ross was so relived.

All that time wondering what Laura was going to say.

He had not thought about her being pregnant.

'I must admit' he said to Laura.

'You did keep me in suspense, I was wondering what you were going, to say to me'.

'I know' she said laughing 'if only you could have seen the look on, your face'.

"We'll meet up for a meal with your parents and your dad and tell, them together" Ross suggested.

"Sounds like a good idea to me' said Laura.

"Now sit down and put your feet up and I'm cooking tonight' demanded Ross.

"Stop fussing Ross' laughed Laura

"I am quite capable of cooking."

"You've had a long flight why don't you go have a shower."

"Then we'll eat and have the rest of the evening to catch up."

Ross pulled Laura into his arms.

"I love you Mrs. Portland and baby Portland."

"Wonder if it will be a boy or a girl' he asked.

"Well Ross it'll be one or the other' she giggled.

'Now go and get in that shower' she told him.

Laura phoned her dad and Ross phoned his parents to, arrange a meal out together.

They asked Josie to join them.

She made the excuse she had made other arrangements.

Of course, she was going to spend the weekend with Jimmy.

After all she wasn't aware that Laura was pregnant.

They choose a nice quiet restaurant.

Half way through evening Ross ordered a bottle of champagne, Laura ordered an orange juice.

They all wondered what they were going to celebrate.

"We have something to tell you all' Ross told them,

He squeezed Laura's hand

"Laura and I are going to have an addition to the family"

'So raise your glasses to us and the future grandparents."

Congratulations were heard all round the table and glasses were raised.

"When is the baby due Laura?" asked Ross's mum Mary.
"September' she answered

"It's so exciting for you both" said Mary.

Laura could see the look on her dad's face she knew what he was thinking.

He was happy for her, but wishing her mum was there to,
Share the joy of it all.

Laura leaned over towards him and squeezed his hand.

"Never know we might have another champ in the family'
Said Laura.

"You make sure you look after yourself' said Charlie.
'She will I'll see to that don't you worry' replied Ross.

The men talked about cars and golf most of the evening.
Laura and Mary were discussing shopping for baby items.

'Of course I would like to buy the pram if that's alright with you'
asked Charlie to Phillip and Mary.
'A wonderful suggestion' replied Mary.

'Make sure it's got a good chassis' said Phillip laughing.

'You don't have to dad' commented Laura.
'I know I don't', but it's what your mother would have wanted,
replied Charlie.

'That's settled it' interrupted Ross.
'Thank you Charlie from us both.

Chapter 14

Ross couldn't wait to tell Jimmy he was going to be a dad.
The next morning Ross got up early and phoned to tell Jimmy the news.

"Guess what?' he said."

"I know you had a bad dream, and wet the bed" Jimmy sarcastically, replied.

"Cheeky bugger, no I'm going to be a dad "said Ross.
"Congratulations, we'll have to wet the baby's head",

Jimmy replied.

Laura had asked Mary to help decorate the baby's room.
Mary painted animal murals on the nursery bedroom walls.

They spent many days out together buying furniture and baby clothes.

The pram was chosen, but Laura refused to have it delivered until, nearer her time.

Although Laura was not the superstitious type she used to say that it, was all a load of rubbish.

The day came for the arrival of baby Portland.

As Laura stepped out of the shower she felt a sharp pain.

Her waters had broken.

'Ross' she shouted.

"It's time to go to the hospital my waters have broken."

Ross phoned the hospital to let them know they were on, their way.

He flapped about putting the case in the car.

"Stop panicking" demanded Laura as she settled in to the passenger, seat.

"I'm the one having the baby'

Ross was weaving in and out of the traffic.

"Slow down' you'll have an accident before we get to hospital Ross', Laura said.

"Well we can't have you giving birth in the car' Ross replied.

Laura arrived safely at the hospital.

Ross jumped out the car.

He rushed to the passenger side opening the door to help Laura get, out.

"Carefully does it," he told her.

"Save your energy, you'll need it for later she said."

Come this way Mrs. Portland said the midwife let's get you settled and, check you progress.

When the time came for Laura to give birth,

Ross gowned up for the delivery room.

He wanted to be there by Laura's side.

Laura was sweating and felt exhausted between contractions.

You can mop your wife's brow the midwife told Ross.

Ross placed the wet cloth across her brow with a feeling of, guilt his wife was in so much pain.

One more push said the midwife I can see the baby's head.

Laura gave a groan as she pushed for the last time.

After a few hours of labour the baby had arrived safely.

You have a lovely baby boy informed the midwife.

The baby let out a load cry.

He's got a good set of lungs as well. She commented.

Ross was so excited, a boy.

He leaned over and kissed Laura on the forehead.

I'm so proud of you he said to Laura.

I can't believe I'm a dad' he beamed with excitement.

The nurse cut the umbilical cord, wiped the baby's face and handed, him to Laura.

She held him tight and kissed his forehead.

Such a tiny thing said Laura.

Ross starred in amazement at them both.

The nurse took the baby from Laura to weigh him then freshened up, his little body.

She wrapped him in a clean blanket to keep him warm.

Laura was taken from the delivery room and settled in a private room, on the ward.

The cot was at the side of the bed ready for when the nurse brought, the baby to her.

When the nurse entered the room she passed the baby to Laura.

He weighed 3.714 Kg the midwife said to them both.

(8lbs 3oz) converted commented Ross.

'Have you decided what you're going to call him?

Asked the nurse?

'Laura looked up at Ross, 'James' she replied.

'A lovely name for him' said the nurse.

"Do you want to hold your son" Laura asked Ross.

"I might drop him' said Ross looking worried.

"Of course you won't, you'll have to get used to it'.

Ross bent down and lifted him out of Laura's arms.

Gently cradling his son.

He couldn't take his eyes off him he took in his squidgy little nose; he counted 10 fingers, and 10 toes.

There was not much hair.

Then James started to cry, Ross handed him back to Laura.

'Expect he's hungry' she said to Ross.

Ross sat there looking at him suckling at her breast.

After she had feed him she laid him in his cot.

'You look tired' Laura said to Ross.

'Tired you're the one who needs the rest' he commented.

'Why don't you phone your mum and dad to let them know they, have a grandson' questioned Laura.

'Whilst you're doing that I'll phone my dad'.

Laura was so excited waiting for her dad to answer the phone.
Charlie picked up his phone saw it was Laura's number.
He was wondering if everything was alright.
 "Guess what, what did I say about having another champ in the, family?"
"You have a grandson "she told her dad.
He replied "I'm so proud of you Laura, are you alright, and the baby, what did he weigh?'
3.714 Kg Laura said laughing.
 In other words "8lb 3oz a good weight Laura told him.
 Why didn't you say that in the first place commented Charlie?
 Laura knew what her dad was like old fashioned when it,
 came to weight conversions in kilo grams.
 Have you and Ross decided on a name yet?' her dad asked.
 "Well we thought James has it's yours and Ross's middle names',
"good choice" he replied.
 "Now you get some rest I'll speak to you tomorrow.
 He instructed Laura.
 'OK dad love you bye for now" she said.
'Love you too, he replied.
 Ross phoned his parents and broke the news to them.
 They were so excited, a grandson they couldn't wait to tell Josie the, wonderful news.
 "When is Laura and baby James expecting to come home' Mary asked, Ross.
 "Tomorrow' replied Ross.
"Send them both our love and we can't wait to see them both"
 "OK mum will do' or, should I say grandma or nana,' Laughed Ross.
 "Grandma I think it's got a nice sound to it' she told Ross.
'Ok bye mum I'll let you know when they are both home'.
 He walked back to the ward to see Laura and James.

He noticed Laura was dozing off.

James lay peacefully asleep in his cot.

"You get some rest now love and I'll be back here early in the morning; to take you two homes' he told her.

He gave her and James a kiss.

Ross left the hospital and drove home thinking all the time about his, son.

Such a tiny little thing how fragile it felt to hold him.

Also he wondered if he would be a good father.

Mary phoned Josie to break the news she was an auntie now.

The house was buzzing with excitement.

'Well' were grandparents' said Mary.

'It will seem strange having a baby around the house again.

I can't wait to hold him" she told Phillip.

'Yes' said Phillip, continuing' I wonder if he'll take after Ross with a, golf club in his hand'.

Mary looked at him in amusement.

"Oh for goodness' sake he's only just been born.

Let him grow up first.

"Only wondering that's all said Phillip laughing.

I'm putting the kettle on' said Mary 'do you want a cup of tea'.

"Haven't we got anything stronger to wet the baby's head?" asked, Phillip.

'Yes but I'm having a cup of tea' Said Mary.

'You can get a drink if you want to'.

Ross got up early to tidy the house before going to fetch Laura and, his son from hospital.

A son, it still felt strange saying 'my son'.

Ross rushed to answer the phone.

 "Ross its Jimmy sorry I was out last night so I missed your call'.
'What's the matter?'
"I was phoning to tell you that I'm a dad' Laura gave birth to a boy."
 "Congratulations "said Jimmy "what are you going to call him.
"James' replied Ross, "well sounds good to me" said Jimmy'.
 The drinks are on me next time."
 "You're right I'll let you know when" Said Ross.
 "I'm just going to hospital to bring Laura and James home".
 'I'll catch up later."He said.
"Ok drive safely and send my love to them both "said Jimmy.

Ross was cursing putting the baby seat in the car.
"Gets better with practice" said Laura.
"Jolly well hope so or he'll be on the sunroof.
 Only joking" He smiled.
"Well I can't wait to get home' was Laura's reply 'and settle James into,
his new room."
 Ross drove home steadily, conscious of the newborn baby in the car,
with them.
As he pulled up in the drive he rushed round to the passenger seat to,
help Laura out.
"I'm not an invalid' she laughed' just get James out of the car he will,
soon wake for a feed." She told him.
"You need to get some rest as soon as we get in," Ross told her.
 "Don't want you tiring yourself out he might keep you up all night."
 "What do you mean', what about you taking your turn to feed him' she
told him.
"I will you know what I mean' said Ross.
 "Just testing' said Laura" making sure you're going to do your bit."
 Laura walked into the kitchen laughing does he know what he's let,
himself in for she thought.

They settled James in his room he seemed content in his cot.

Ross stood looking at him mesmerized at this tiny human being. Thinking of all the things they would be able to do together as he was, growing up.

We can go golfing, fishing, he said talking to James.

Laura turned round to face Ross.

"Wait a minute,' she said 'how do you know he'd like to do those, sorts of things."

"Of course he would he's a boy isn't he'.

So! Asked Laura

"He might want to play with dolls".

"Not bloody likely said Ross."

"He might be into other things,"

Laura smiled go on with you she said to Ross.

They checked the baby alarm was set to on.

Then they quietly crept out the room so as not to disturb him.

Laura sank down in the arm chair exhausted.

Ross sorted out the cooking.

Laura's mind was on other things.

She knew Ross would be away in two weeks time.

So little time for him, she thought to have with her and James.

But that was what it was like being a professional golfer.

Knowing what her mother put up with when her dad was away so, much of the time.

He was no sooner home then off to the next tournament.

Still she knew only too well what she had taken on they had talked, about it so much before they were married.

"Lunch is ready shouted Ross."

"OK I'm coming" Laura replied she tucked into the lovely meal.

"That was very tasty, you can do the entire cooking if every meal is as, good as that one' she told him.

"Well enjoy it while I'm here, I've got to look after you two'.

"Anyway you need a rest so put your feet up and I'll clear up and we'll enjoy sometime together before his nibs wakes up for a feed."

"No sooner had he said that James started to stir."

"Think I spoke to soon' he said.

Laura fed James and settled him down.

As they sat together Ross was discussing inviting the parents and, Josie over before he went away.

He suggested inviting them over for Sunday lunch.
That will give us a few days to have together to spend some time alone, with James.

It's important we have this time the three of us.
I'm sure all the grandparents will want to see baby James.'
He said.

Later that day Ross spoke to his parents on the phone and made the, arrangements for Sunday lunch.

They told him that they were as excited as he was to see James.

They all agreed that the new parents needed some time together on, their own, so Sunday lunch sounded lovely.

They also told him they would have plenty of time to help, Laura and enjoy their new grandchild whilst Ross was away.

The phone rang Laura leaned over to pick it up to answer.
"How's my grandson?' asked a voice on the other end"

"What about your daughter' Laura asked her dad.
"Do I take second place?" She laughed.
"James is doing very well, though I mustn't speak to soon."

"Not keeping you up to much in the night 'asked her Dad.
"He's settled better than I thought can't complain at this moment'.
'I was just going to phone you' she told him.

"Ross's parents are coming for lunch on Sunday and we'll expect you, to unless you have other plans?

'Other plans, he said.
"The only plans I have is seeing my grandson grow up."
"Well in that case we'll see you on Sunday can't wait.

"Okay love, you make sure you get plenty of rest."
"Yes dad' Ross is running around cooking and cleaning she explained.
'I'll miss him when he's away' she told her Dad.

''I know you will' but we're all here for you, so don't try to do,
everything yourself when we can help' her dad told her.
Don't want you tiring yourself out when Ross is away.
"You know what it was like for me and your mum" he said.
"I know' sighed Laura, 'we'll be ok doing worry."
    Laura said her goodbye and knew she couldn't wait for her dad to see,
his baby grandson James.

Chapter 15

The days went too quickly for them both.

Sunday had come and everyone had arrived to see James.

Mary helped Ross with the Sunday roast.

Charlie and Phillip were wetting the baby's head.

Josie enjoyed taking James for a walk.

They all insisted Laura had a rest in the afternoon.

Ross took several photographs of the grandparents and Josie with, baby James.

Then he set the camera up to take a family group together.

When it was time to leave, they all gave Laura instructions.

She was to phone any time day and night if she needed any help, while Ross was away.

Mary was only too pleased to look after James any time, she told her.

This eased Ross's mind whilst he was away from home.

Ross was back and forth on his tours.

James was growing up and had started nursery.

Laura had returned to work.

Charlie spent a lot of time enjoying his grandson.

Laura loved to see them in the garden together.

Mary would have James over to sleep some weekends.

This gave Laura some time to catch up with her friends for coffee.

The year had flown by.

James was coming up to his second birthday and would be, celebrating with some of his friends from nursery and family.

Laura used to say he was spoilt.

Every time Ross went on tour he would buy a toy at the airport to bring, home for James.

Ross tried to spend as much time as he could with James and, Laura when he was at home.

He knew family life was precious to him.

James had brought so much joy to him.

Charlie loved spoiling his grandson

Christmas was only two weeks away.

Charlie had brought him an electric train set.

Laura questioned her dad 'is this for James or for you' she said, laughing.

James helped his mum decorate the tree.

He was so excited.

When Christmas day came they all turned up at Ross and Laura's, house for the day.

James had that many presents he didn't know who's to open next.

His mum and dad had brought him a pedal car.

Ross laughed when Phillip said he should have got one with an engine, in.

They all had a wonderful day.

Ross had enjoyed the days off with his family.

The New Year was looming.

He wondered what that would bring for them all.

Ross was packed and ready to leave on the Monday morning.

He would be taking the 2-30 flight to South Carolina for the next, tournament and would be away for a week.

'Have you got everything, tickets, passport, Laura asked him.

Don't fuss' he said to Laura 'you just look after yourself and my little, boy.

Mum's coming over this afternoon to help'.

Ross stood on the door step, part of him wanted to go but the other, part didn't he hated leaving them both.

Especially as James was growing up so fast, he'd missed his first steps, he'd taken his first tooth he got.

He was growing up so fast he'll soon be getting ready to start school, thought Ross.

He wanted to have more time with them.

Jimmy pulled up in the drive.

He had the car window down and the radio on blaring out the latest, hits in the charts.

He hooted his horn "Coming" shouted Ross.

Ross put his clubs and case in the car.

He gave James a hug and kissed Laura goodbye.

"Look after yourself" he told her.

"I'll phone you when we've arrived at the hotel 'he said.

Don't forget what the others have said about asking for help.

'I won't' replied Laura.

Ross fastened his seat belt then they were on their way.

Jimmy pulled out the drive.

Pipping the horn and waving goodbye.

Ross glanced around and blew them a kiss.

Ross and Jimmy's caddie would meet them at the airport.

They arrived in plenty of time for checking in their cases and, golf clubs.

They would have time to have a drink before they boarded the plane.

Ross glanced around looking for Jimmy.

As usual he was chatting up the hostess ladies.

'You're supposed to be checking in not chatting the women, up' said Ross.

'Alright keep your hair on' Jimmy replied.

The look on Dills face said it all.

Dill and Big Joe just laughed.

Their flight number was called for them to board the plane.

They settled in their seats.

The engines started all the safety checks had been done they were, on their way.

The hostess lady was pushing her trolley loaded up with drinks.

She was a Pretty girl and looked very smart in her uniform.

When she stopped at Jimmy's seat she turned and looked at him.
"Can I get you anything 'she asked?"
Jimmy's mind wasn't on the drink.
 He looked her up and down.
 Ross nudged him with his elbow saying,
 "Jimmy the lady is asking you if you want a drink 'don't be rude,
answer her.'
 "Oh sorry "Jimmy replied 'I was miles away'.
 Realizing what he had said, he laughed out load.
 'Well we really are miles away'.
 He told the air hostess 'I'll have a whisky and soda please'
 'Anything else' she asked.
He hesitated, what now thought Ross?
'No thanks' that will be all' he replied.
With that she severed him his drink.
Reaching out to take the glass Jimmy thanked her.
 She looked at Ross "Can I get you a drink sir?"
'Yes please I'll have the same that's all' replied Ross.
 She prepared the drink then passed it to him.
Ross thanked her.
 As the air hostess moved further down the aisle.
Ross looked at jimmy.
 'For goodness sake jimmy can't you leave it alone for one minute?
Ross snapped.
 What do you mean? Jimmy asked him.
 'You know very well what I mean' said Ross.
"I don't know what you're talking about "replied Jimmy.
"You can't fool me Jimmy I've known you too long Ross told him.
 "No harm in looking" Jimmy responded.
 "Isn't that what you always say it must be your favourite line?
 With that they both settled down put their head phones on and tuned in,
to the TV.

There flight landed on time and the taxi driver was waiting to load the, bags and clubs in the car.

 A few minutes later and they were on their way to the hotel.

  After the flight and car journey they were impatient to get to their, hotel.

  The door man was waiting for them as the car pulled up at the hotel.

  The luggage was taken to their rooms whilst they both signed in.
Dill and Big Joe sorted out the golf clubs.

 Then they would make their way to their rooms to freshen up before, the evening meal.

  The receptionist informed them that the evening meals will be served, from 6-30 onwards.

 The receptionist asked the guest if there was any question's or, anything else she could assist with.

  Ross waited in anticipation for Jimmy to say something.
"No that will be all thank you" Jimmy told her.

 Thank goodness for that thought Ross.

 After all they would be there for four days.

 He wanted to enjoy his stay as well as his golf.

  "I'll see you at dinner' said Jimmy who was off for shower and lay, down before the meal."
'Sounds like a good idea to me catch up later' Ross replied.

Chapter 16

Ross unpacked his case took a shower and lay on the bed thinking, about Laura and James.

How he missed them.

He looked at the clock the time difference would be late evening.

He could make a quick call to let Laura know he had arrived safely.

Laura answered the phone.

"Hello love, how are you both?' asked Ross.

"I've been thinking about you' he told her.

"We're fine', did you have a good flight?' asked Laura.

Ross told her the flight was fine.

'Has James settled for the night'? He asked.

'Yes' she replied, then she went on to explain that James had been, into mischief with Auntie Josie you know what she's like with him.

Ross gave out a hearty laugh.

He's a typical boy' he replied.

Anyway don't you worry about us you just concentrate on your game, and bring us back a trophy "She instructed him?

"I'll try' he responded.

'You take care, love you and miss you' said Ross.

"Me too, bye love speak to you tomorrow' Laura said.

Ross switched off the mobile and got ready to go for his evening meal.

They were looking forward to playing the course.

It was renowned for the view of the sea and fast, undulated greens.

There were several water hazards that they had to contend with and, bunkers around the greens.

Ross looked at Jimmy and thought; I'd better get some practice in if, I'm going to beat him.

They still had that edge of competitiveness between them.

The tournament was played over 4 days.

The competition had been tight on the score board through the, tournament.

They had both played well in fact Ross had won by only one shot, ahead of the other players.

Dill was in his element, Ross had won another tournament.

He knew he would be getting a good bonus.

Ross couldn't wait to phone Laura to tell her the news that he would, be coming home with another trophy.

Laura was excited not only because he had won.

But he would be on the early morning flight back home.

She couldn't wait to see him, not just for her but for James also.

The flight had been delayed by a couple of hours.

So Ross walked around the duty free looking for some perfume to take, home for Laura.

He spotted a toy elephant on a stand, when you wound it up the, elephants trunk rose up, the ears flapped up and down, and its legs, moved, as he picked it up the young lady at the counter commented to, him how cute it was.

"I'll take it" he said my little boy will love this as he paid for the, items.

Ross crammed the items in his bag.

"Looks like you've been spending your money" Commented Jimmy.

'Yes it will be a nice surprise for them' he told Jimmy.

Ross and Jimmy were annoyed about the two hour delay.

The landing of the plane was a little bumpy on touch down on the, runway.

Neither of them was in a good mood.

They were both tired from the hanging around at the airport and the, long flight.

Getting through customs seemed to take ages.

Jimmy collected his car; they loaded up the cases and clubs.

They were on their way home.
Jimmy was weaving in and out of the traffic.
'What's the rush' asked Ross.
'You'll get us both killed, slow down Jimmy.'
You're doing ninety and there's a limit on the carriageway.
Ross told him.
"Well we want to get home; we've been hanging about long enough."
Jimmy told Ross.
"Yes, but in one piece" Replied Ross.
Jimmy turned off into a side road.
'I don't want to tell you how to drive' Said Ross.
'But this is at narrow road with some sharp bends.
So take your time'.

Jimmy was getting annoyed with Ross commenting all the time,
about his driving he put his foot down.
'Were coming to a sharp bend Jimmy you're going too fast snapped,
Ross.
Jimmy took his eye off the road for a second to look at Ross.
'Have you finished' Jimmy said 'all you have done is criticize my,
bloody driving, what's the matter with you?
'Look out 'Screamed Ross.
Suddenly Jimmy swerved to miss the oncoming van.
The car careered off the road and rolled down the bank hitting a tree.
The van driver ran down the road shouting at Jimmy about his,
driving.
When he got to the car he could see what a mess it was in, and called,
the ambulance and fire brigade.
By the looks of it all they would need both.
The passenger side was smashed against a tree.
The van driver looked into the car.
'What the hell were you doing' he asked Jimmy.
'You were driving way too fast 'he said.
Jimmy looked up at him in a daze, he had cuts to his head the blood,
running down his face and his ribs were hurting him.

'How's your friend', the van driver ask as he tried to arouse him.

Ross was unconscious and his arm was trapped blood was pouring, down his arm.

'I've called the ambulance and fire brigade' the van driver told Jimmy.

By the time the ambulance crew arrived Jimmy had got out of the, car.

The paramedic helped him into the ambulance.

Two other paramedics were assessing Ross's injuries.

This guy is hurt quite bad they said.

They worked on him trying to stem the bleeding.

Doing all they could to keep him alive they manage to get Ross stable,

The fire brigade arrived and they discussed the damage.

'We're going to have to cut the roof off' they told the paramedics.

They instructed the ambulance crew to keep the passenger stable, while they assessed the situation, and inform them if his condition, started to deteriorate.

They commented that they needed to get him out the car as quickly as, possible.

The fire crew cut the roof off, making access for the paramedics to, get Ross out as carefully as they could.

They placed him on a stretcher.

The crew radioed for emergency assistance on arrival at the hospital.

The sirens were going.

The medics took details from Jimmy regarding Ross's next of kin.

On arrival at the hospital Ross was rushed in to the emergency bay, and assessed by the doctors in charge.

They knew he had to go to theatre urgently as he had lost a lot of, blood and had a badly damaged injury to his arm.

He also had injuries to his ribs and leg.

Jimmy gave Ross's details to the nurses so they could contact Laura.
The nurse attended to Jimmy's injuries.
Jimmy was slight concussed.
She advised him he would be transferred to the ward for twenty four,
hour observation.
   Laura was busy in the kitchen when the phone rang.
   She was wondering if it was Ross phoning to say he was on his way,
home.
   She was in a state of shook when she got the phone call from the,
hospital about Ross.
   She was shaking and sobbing her heart out when she phoned her dad.
   Answering the phone Charlie asked her 'What's the matter love' '
'Oh dad' she said, 'the hospital just phoned, Ross has been in a car,
accident can you come over and drive me to the hospital',
'I'm on my way' Charlie quickly replied.
 Charlie grabbed his coat and car keys.
Locked up the house and headed to Laura's.
   She quickly made arrangements for a friend to look after James.
Laura was anxious to see Ross and find out the extent of his injuries,
   She phoned Ross's parents to tell them about the accident they told,
her they would meet her at the hospital.
Charlie drove up to the front door.
 Laura stood there, tears streaming down her cheeks.
 She was waiting with a bag packed with James clothes.
 Charlie got out the car 'do you know what happened'   he asked her.
   'No' she replied but it sounds as though Ross is in a bad way'.
Charlie put his arms around her' come on love' he said, as he picked,
James up 'let's get this young man in his seat.'
   They dropped James off at Angie's Laura's friend.
   'Don't worry about James he'll be fine you've got enough to cope,
with' said Angie,
Laura gave her a peck on the cheek.
 'I'll call you when I get to the hospital and let you know what's,
happening. She replied.

She gave James a kiss,' now you be a good boy for Auntie Angie' she, told him.

They were on their way to the hospital.

Laura rushed through the hospital doors and went to the reception, area.

'I'm Laura Portland, my husband Ross was in a car accident' she said.

Come with me instructed the reception lady.

I'll take you to the waiting room where you can speak to the sister in, charge' she told Laura.

They stood in the room every minute seemed like hours.

Laura feared the worse for Ross.

Charlie tried to console her.

A few minutes later the door opened and in walked a short stocky, nurse.

Hello I'm Sister Rose she told Laura.

She gestured them to take a seat.

I'm sorry to have to tell but, you're husband was in a bad way when, he arrived here.

We had to take him straight to theatre.

Laura gasped and started to panic, 'how badly injured was he' she, asked Sister Rose.

I'm afraid I can't answer that at this moment we will know more, when he's out off surgery.

In the meantime can I get you both a cup of tea? She asked.

Laura asks Sister Rose if she knew where the driver of the car is, 'Yes he's in the casualty bay being attended to'.

She informed Laura.

'Can you take me to him?' asked Laura' I need to talk to him.

'I'm afraid you will have to wait until the doctor's have, finished attending to him first' responded Sister Rose.

'I'll let him know you have arrived'. She told Laura.

With that she left to arrange a tray of tea for them both.

'Come on love' said Charlie. 'You've got to be strong for Ross'.
He put his arm around her as she burst into tears.

'Oh dad why did this happen' she cried.
What are we going to do? She asks him.
'What about Ross I don't want to lose him'.
Charlie stood there supporting his daughter.
No matter what he said it wouldn't change what had happened.
All he could do was to be there for Laura and wanted to know how it, had happened.
Ross's parents met Laura and Charlie in the hospital.
'What happened' Mary and Phillip asked.
Mary was in a state of shock; Phillip tried to console her,
Mary walked over to Laura and put her arms around her.

All Charlie and Phillip could do was to say 'we'll find out what, happened don't you worry'.
'Someone has got to answer to this'.
Mary asked if Laura had spoken to the doctor yet.

'Not yet' she told Mary she explained that they were waiting for the, surgeon to come out of theatre.
Then they could find out the extent of the injuries and what happens, next.
'Who's looking after James' asked Mary
'He's staying with Angie' she's offered to help and do whatever she, can' replied Laura.
She's a good friend of mine and has a little girl' Laura said.
'Dad's going to stay at my house for the time being'.
Mary asked her about Jimmy.
Laura told her that he escaped with minor injuries, cuts to his head and, hands and some bruised ribs, but not as extensive as Ross's injuries, nothing like Ross' they had heard.
Josie had arrived at the hospital and was questioning what had, happened.
She was not only concerned for Ross but for Jimmy also.

An hour had passed by and Jimmy had been seen by the doctor.
Jimmy was slightly concussed besides his other injuries.
The doctor had admitted him to the ward for twenty four hour,
observation

The sister came back to see Laura and the family to tell them they,
could see him for a short while.

Chapter 17

As they walked into the ward they could see the pain in,
Jimmy's face,
 'I'm sorry' said Jimmy as soon as he saw them as tears,
Came to his eyes.
'What happened?' asked Charlie.
Jimmy said he wasn't aware of the sharp bend.
He had just taken his eye off the road for a split second.
He had to swerve to miss a van coming from the opposite,
direction the car careered off the road, it rolled down the,
 bank and hit the tree.
Ross took the brunt force of the accident on his side of the car.
Charlie asked Jimmy if he was driving too fast.
He knew what Jimmy was like when he got behind the wheel.
 Jimmy more or less admitted he may have been too fast,
for the condition of the road.
By that time Charlie's blood was boiling.
 'Bloody fool, you nearly killed Ross' Charlie remarked.
Laura kept asking him questions she wanted to know exactly what
had, happened.
 Josie arrived and stood there frozen for a second aware of the tension.
She did not want anyone to know that she had been seeing Jimmy.
After all this was not the time or place.
    Everyone was angry about Jimmy's driving.
The last thing they needed to know was that she was involved with,
him.
Josie walked out the room and clasped her head in her hands,
 to stop the tears flowing down her face.

After Laura and the family had left Jimmy's room she slipped back in, to see him.

She leaned over and kissed Jimmy, he took Josie by the hand.

'Sorry Josie' he said to her.

'Please forgive me I didn't mean for any of this to happen'.

'Ross and I were arguing in the car before it happened 'he told Josie.

'Please don't say anything to the family' he asked her.

'It's such a mess' replied Josie.

'Ross was in such a bad way they had to take him straight to theatre', Josie told him.

After all it was her brother in theatre.

'What was it you and Ross were arguing about' she asked him.

'My driving' replied Jimmy.

What with the delayed flight and hanging about at the airport we were, both tired I just wanted to get home'.

'Ross was going on and on about my driving I'd had enough of it'.

'I wasn't aware of the sharp bend it happened in a flash' Jimmy said.

I swerved to miss the van the car skidded off the road careered down, the bank it hit a tree on the passenger side, he told her.

'What were you thinking about Jimmy' said Josie to him 'you should, have been more careful with your driving then all this wouldn't have, happened.'

I can't imagine what state Ross must have been in to have had to cut, the roof off the car to get him out.

Jimmy could only say over and over again 'I'm sorry'.

Josie gave Jimmy a hug, then he told her to go and see Laura.

'Your family will be wondering what's going on' he told her.

'Yes' said Josie 'I'll phone you later.

'I will let you know how Ross is when he comes out of theatre', she said to him.

Josie left and returned to see Laura and the rest of the family.

The minutes ticked by slowly,
The longer Ross was in theatre the more concerned they all were.
Josie knew she had to say something to them about what Jimmy had, told her about the accident.
Josie told them part of what Jimmy had told her about Ross arguing in, the car with Jimmy.
Also they were both annoyed about the delayed flight they were both, tired and wanted to get home.
'Well that's his side of the story' said Charlie.
'Let's see what Ross has to say about it all. He commented.

Ross had finally come out off surgery and was in recovery.
The Surgeon arrived with Sister Rose to speak to Laura.
Mr Turner introduced himself to Laura and the family.
He informed Laura that once her husband was out of recovery and, settled in intensive care then she could go to see him.

He went on to explain of Ross's injures on admission and the urgency, of taking him straight to theatre.
Laura sat in the chair trying to take in what he was saying.
Mr Turner asked Sister Rose if she could arrange some tea for them all.
She called the nurse and asked her to arrange refreshments for them, all.
'Is there anything else'? she asked Laura.
Laura would like to have said 'Yes my husband in one piece' but, replied 'no just tea thank you.
We could all do with something stronger than a cup of tea thought, Charlie.
'I'll be in my office if you need me' Mr Turner told Sister Rose.
'Very well' Mr Turner came her reply.
Ross parents were as anxious as Laura about Ross's injuries and knew, she would take priority to seeing him.
Time would be limited to visiting him in intensive care.

Chapter 18

Mr Turner returned to see Laura.

'Mrs. Portland' your husband's is out of recovery and is being, transferred into intensive care' He told her.

We'll get him settled then you can go in and see him.

He told her he was sedated so may drift in and out of sleep.

'Your husband had several injuries, 'not only had he fractured some, ribs and deep cuts to his leg'.

He had serious injuries to his arm and neck area.

He explained the type of injury to Laura, Brachial plexus.

'What's that' asked Laura.

I'm afraid he had extensive damages to his nerves in his,
 neck and shoulder area this will affect his arm and hand.

I had to do a nerve graft from his leg.

Laura stood there in a trance.

She couldn't take it in what he was saying.

I'm sorry Mrs. Portland said Mr. Turner'.

I know it must be a shock to you.

He's sedated he also lost a lot of blood so we had to give him a, transfusion.

Will he be able to play golf again? replied Laura.

We can talk more about his injuries later Mr Turner told Laura.

I'm sure you would like to see your husband now'.

He answered.

The sister arrived to let Laura know Ross was settled and she could,
go in and see him.

Laura stood at the bedside looking at all the equipment.

She leaned over and kissed Ross on the forehead.

All she could do was stare at him lying there with all the tubing,
connected to him wishing this wasn't happening, her mind in a daze.

She looked across at his arm all bandages up with a,

Sling brace for support.

He may drift in and out of sleep the nurse told Laura.

She noticed Laura was looking at the bag of blood connected,
to the machine, being transfused into Ross body.

'He lost a lot of blood 'The nurse told Laura.

She carried on saying he may drift in and out of sleep.

But Laura could stay as long as she wanted to.

Laura watched as the nurses carried on with their duties.

After a short time she went to see Ross's parents and her dad and,
updated them of his condition.

She asked the nurses if his parents and Josie could see him.

Laura stayed with her dad to let Ross's family have some time with,
Ross.

They stayed a short time knowing they needed to let the,
nurses do their work.

Laura's mind went on to James wondering what he was doing,
at Angie's.

Angie had a little girl Emily she was 6yrs old.

She loved to see James they played well together.

Angie used to say to Laura their like sister and brother.

After a while Ross's family let Laura return to see Ross with,
her dad.

It was getting late they knew there was nothing more they,
could do, and they were tired it had been a long day for them,
all, so they decided to go home.

They knew Laura would let them know of any changes to,
Ross condition.

The sister came to see Laura.

She could tell looking at Laura she was anxious and tired.

"Why don't you go home and get some rest "she suggested.

"I know you want to be here but there's nothing you can do,
  at this moment."

'He's in good hands; you can come what time you would like,
tomorrow.

'His condition is stable and we will phone you if there are,
  any changes.

  The sister put her arm around Laura to comfort her,

  Laura agreed she needed to get some rest, she was tired and knew she,
would need all the strength she had to get through this.

  'Come on Love' said Charlie 'let's take you home'.

Laura thanked the Sister and nurses for all they were doing.

Then left them to carrying on with their work.

Laura tried to settle for the night.

  But it was hard for her, knowing Ross was lay there and everyone,
unaware of what the surgeon was going to say about the future for,
Ross due to his injuries.

  Her mind kept going back to the accident.

She kept imagining what terrible condition Ross must have been in,
when it happened to have to be rushed into surgery.

It didn't bear thinking about she could have lost him.

  The thought of it unnerved her panic set in she burst in to tears.

She was terrified of what the consequences were going to be,
  for Ross.

  Laura woke early the next morning she was worrying if Ross had,
comfortable night.

  She wanted to phone the hospital but knew it was the early hours of,
the morning.

  She went down stairs and made herself a cup of coffee.

Although the sister did say she could phone anytime.

She looked at the clock it was 6-30 she couldn't wait any longer,

She picked up her mobile and pressed in the numbers.

'Hello' she said to the nurse,' its Mrs. Portland can you tell me how, my husband is please?

The nurses filled her in on Ross's condition.

I'll be in later this morning' she told the nurse on the phone.

At 7-30am Charlie woke up and showered.

When he came down the stairs Laura was already on the phone to, Angie.

'Are you sure you don't mind having James'? she asked.

'Of Course not' came the reply, in times like these what are friends for, you have enough to cope with'.

'He'll be ok don't you worry about him you just look after yourself,' Angie told her.

'Thanks Angie I'll call you later' said Laura.

Charlie was wondering who Laura was talking to thinking it may have, been the hospital.

'Who's that you were on the phone to love' he asked her.

'Angie' Laura answered.

'I was just wondering how James was' she replied.

James has been as good as gold, settling at Angie's overnight'.

"She is going to look after him again today' she told her dad.

"That's good of her" said Charlie.

'Now you try and eat something'.

'By the way dad', Laura said 'I phoned the hospital earlier to see what, sort of night Ross had.

'The nurse said he had been comfortable.

'I did let her know we would be in later this morning',

'That's good news love' Charlie said to her.

Laura phoned Ross's parents to let them know she had spoken to the, nurse that morning to enquire at what sort of night Ross had she also, told them her dad would be taking her in later that morning.

Mary, Phillip, and Josie would be arriving midday.

A couple of hours later Charlie and Laura arrived at the hospital.
Mr Turner was waiting in his office.

Knowing he would have to go into more detail with Laura, regarding,
her husband's injuries.
Laura had requested for her dad to be there also, to listen to what,
Mr. Turner had to say.

He invited them into his office and asked them both to take a seat.
Mr Turner braced himself.

He went on to say, 'As I told you yesterday Mrs. Portland.
Your husband injuries I'm afraid were very bad'.
'He not only had fractured some ribs'.
'He lost a lot of blood, so we had to give him a transfusion'.
'He had damaged the nerves to his neck and arm',
'The nerves were very badly damaged'
'A complete Brachial Plexus'.
This may result in loss of use in his arm and grip in his left,
Hand it may be permanently.
I had to take a skin graft from the Sural Nerve in his leg.
He had deep cuts to his left leg'
He went on to say unfortunately it is a slow recovery process.
'Please explain what this means to his recovery' Asked Laura,
confused.

Mr Turner explained about physiotherapy that Ross would undertake,
and suggested ways in which they could assist,

With Ross's recovery.
'What about his golf' asked Laura?
I'm afraid to say said Mr Turner this may be the end of his career.
That's all I can say at this moment.

Laura looked at her dad, 'how could this happen golf is his life',
'How am I going to tell him he may never play again'?
Laura asked, 'Let's wait and see' said Charlie.
   'We have to give him time to recover'.
   I'm sorry' said Mr Turner 'I know it must be a difficult time for you,
all'.
'Thank you for being so honest' replied Laura.
   With that Laura and her dad got up from their chair and left,
Mr. Turner's office.
   She was so confused trying to digest all the information in,
   her mind she couldn't believe what had been said.
   'Come on love' said Charlie let's go and see how Ross is.
   They headed for intensive care;
She pushed the door open and entered the room.
   The nurse discussed Ross condition with her.
'He's been comfortable 'she said 'and taking some fluids.
Laura and Charlie took a seat next to the bed.
   She looked across at Ross he looked like a rugby player she thought,
with big muscles noticing all the padding on his shoulder.
   But he was no rugby player, he was a professional golfer.
He had lacerations to his face, swelling below his eyes.
He's still a little drowsy the nurse said to Laura.
   We have given him some morphine to help the pain.
Laura's eyes gazed around the room.
   They focused on the machine recording his observations.
The catheter stand was attached to the bed by what looked,
   Like a large clip device.
   Ross stirred and managed to smile at Laura.
'Hello love' she said as she choked back the tears.
All Ross could do was smile back.
She bent down and kissed and held his hand tightly,
Charlie stood there looking on.
   He could feel the pain that Laura was going through.
He put his hand on her shoulder and gave it a squeeze,

The nurse carried recording Ross's observations.

They stayed by Ross's bed side the rest of the morning.

Mary, Phillip, and Josie arrived in the afternoon to see Ross.

Laura filled them in on what the surgeon had told her, regarding Ross injuries.

There was more to it than the previous conversation she had, with him the night before.

Josie stood there open mouthed when Laura told her Ross, may not be able to play golf again.

Mary's eyes were filled with tears all Phillip could do was, to try and comfort her.

Her son's career had been taken away from him by his best friend. That's what she was thinking.

How was Ross going to manage to live with that?

This is Jimmy's fault Mary said to Phillip.

If he had not been driving that bloody car so fast this would, have never have happened.

Calm down commented Phillip.'

This is not doing Ross any good arguing here.

It was upsetting everyone.

The Nurse suggested they all go for a coffee.

She could feel the tension in the room.

Sorry replied Mary, It's just I don't like to see him lying there, helpless.

Josie put her arms around her mum to comfort her.

Knowing she would slip away at some time during the day and see, Jimmy before he was discharged later that day?

'Why don't you two go and have something to eat.

Mary suggested to Laura and Charlie.

You've been here a while now, having to come in early to see, Mr Turner.

'I don't think I could face anything' commented Laura.

Charlie persuaded Laura to have a bite to eat.

They made their way to the restaurant and left the other's by Ross's, bedside.

Laura returned later with her dad.

By late afternoon Mary and Phillip had decided it was time to leave.

Mary was concerned the worry of it all would bring on another heart, attack for Phillip.

She suggested they both went home so Phillip could have a rest.

Laura understood and agreed with her.

They said their goodbye's to Ross then made their way home.

Josie had left before them to sneak down to the wards to see Jimmy, before he was discharged.

Charlie and Laura stayed until early evening.

She began to doze off in the chair.

'Right young lady' said Charlie 'time to get you home to bed'.

It's been a long day for us both and you need to get a good night's, sleep.

Laura agreed she felt drained it had been an emotional day, for all of them.

Although she knew underneath that there was more to come.

She gave Ross a kiss on the cheek and said, goodnight to him.

They both thanked the nurses for all the care they were giving, to Ross, then headed for the car park.

As they were walking to the car Laura put her arm in her dads.

'Thanks, dad' she said for today.

'What would I do without you by my side'?

'That's what dads are for replied Charlie.

She slipped in to the passenger seat, buckled up her seat belt.

Charlie started up the engine.

The car pulled out the car park they were heading for home.

Angie had arranged with Laura to look after James for, another day.

She knew the day had come for the surgeon to give Ross, the bad news.

How was he going to react to it all thought Angie?

Laura needed all the support she could give her.

Laura was dreading the day as she arrived at the hospital.
Ross had been moved to a private room on the wards.
When she entered the room Ross was sitting up in bed.
His arm was in a sling brace to support his shoulder.
   'The surgeon is coming this morning to see you Ross,
To explain your injuries' Laura told him.
  Ross was feeling very anxious about what the surgeon was going to,
tell him regarding his injuries.
  Laura stared out the window watching the visitors arrive.
  She couldn't look at Ross.
  Knowing what was about to happen.
 Her mind wandered from him to Jimmy.
 She wondered about what Josie had told her about Ross arguing with,
Jimmy before the crash.
  Jimmy must have been driving pretty fast?
  She thought for Ross to end up in this condition.

 The surgeon walked in to the room.
 'Good morning' Mr Portland 'Did you have a comfortable night?
He asked.
Laura turned away from the window to face the surgeon.
 'And good morning to you Mrs. Portland' he said to Laura.
 Mr. Turner pulled up a chair for Laura.
 Take a seat Mrs. Portland' he told her.
  Ross tried to adjust himself to a comfortable position.
 He was waiting in anticipation of what he was going to say.
  Mr Turner explained to Ross the extent of his injury.
 His face turned white.
Laura thought he was going to faint.
She quickly passed him a glass of water.
 Laura had to calm him down he was in shock.
  I know it's not going to be the same for you the surgeon continued.
  You'll have to take one day at a time there's no quick fix.

We can talk about the physiotherapy you will need to do to strengthen,
the muscle in your arm.

  But due to the injury we have to see what limitations you have,
  to your arm'.
'Also you will need to strengthen your good arm.'
 'I'm afraid, playing golf again that may not be possible'.
'We'll give you all the help we can.

  The physiotherapist will come and talk to you, as for regarding
 your sling brace I'm afraid you may have to wear this for,
 Quite some time depending on your recovery it may be permanent.

  Now I suggest you get plenty of rest it's the most important thing,
you can do to help your recovery'.
 I wish I could have given you better news.
  Mr. Turner left the room.

 Ross looked at Laura with a dazed expression on his face.
 Did he hear right.

 He may not be able to play golf again, no more tournaments.
 But that was his life, what was left for him now.
Laura could see the shock on his face,

   The colour drained from him.

   Laura took his hand 'I'm sorry love' she said to him.
'We'll just have to get through this together',
'You need to rest'.

   Does she know what she talking about thought Ross?
 Has she any Idea what this has done to me.
He could not speak; he just had a vacant look on his face trying to,
make sense of what the surgeon had told him.

  Laura sat there for a while trying to comfort him by offering her,
support.

 She knew he had no intentions of making any conversation with her.
He tilted his head to one side looking away from her.
She knew she wasn't getting anywhere with him.
She decided it was time to leave.

Well I'll be off now she said to him.

 I'm going to call in on Angie she's been looking after James for us.

Ross didn't reply to her comment.

She moved the chair back to the corner of the room.

  Moved to the side of the bed and gave him a kiss.

  As she walked to the door she turned around and said to him,

 I'll see you later.

There was no response from Ross.

Laura left feeling empty inside.

Chapter 19

Ross was not thinking about resting.

All he could think about were his golfing years.

How he'd worked hard to get where he was and the trophies he'd won.

Was this it, was there going to be no more?

He thought about the times he'd spent with Jimmy travelling and, having fun with the lads was that going to come to an end?

Laura called in at Angie's on her way home to see James.

Angie's mother answered the door.

''Oh hello Laura come in' she said 'have you come to see James, 'you've just missed him'.

Angie decided to take James and Emily for a walk in the Park.

'She wasn't expecting you to call'.

'I know' replied Laura, 'I just thought I'd pop in and see James before, I go back to the hospital'.

'How's Ross doing'? she asked Laura.

'Angie told me he had been in a bad accident' she commented.

'It must be awful for you all and what a worry'.

Before she could say anymore Laura cut her off

'I'm sorry' Laura said' I have to go will you let Angie Know I, called'.

'I will you take care' came the reply.

Charlie decided to go with Laura to the hospital in the, afternoon.

He visited Ross for a short time then went for a coffee.

Leaving Laura to talk with Ross.

Ross was tired most of the time.
He had hardly eaten anything just a few scoops of Ice cream.
She sat there trying to have a conversation with him.
 She could imagine how he was feeling after the meeting with,
 Mr. Turner devastated.
 'It's alright for him coming here telling me all of this'.
 Ross said to her.
 'How the hell does he know what I'm going through?
Telling me it will take time' he told Laura.
 'He's not the one laying here who's never going to play golf again'.
 'I might just as well not survived the accident what use am I going to,
be' he said to her.
 'Don't say that' replied Laura.
 'Mr. Turner did say it would take time and they would give,
 you all the help they could for recovering'.
 'You have me and a son that's what you have to survive for' she told,
Ross.
 'What good am to you both' answered Ross. '
 Laura brushed the tears from her cheeks.
 It was hard work for her.
 Whatever she said to try and ease the pain for him.
 She couldn't say anything right.
 She needed to get out of the room.
 'I'll phone your parents and let them know the surgeon,
 has spoken to you,' she told Ross
 He didn't care what she did at that moment of time.
 Laura glanced back at him as she walked out the door.
 Wishing it was all a dream but this was for real.
 Phillip and Mary were shocked when she told them the news.
 What was to come of it all they wondered?
 How was Ross going to cope not only physically but,
 Psychologically.

This was all Jimmy's fault, thought Ross.
He's got of lightly compared to me, and he hasn't even,
bothered to come see how I am.
He had warned him about the narrow road, and that he was driving too,
fast coming up to the bend.
Some friend he is he thought as he dozed off to sleep.
Laura meet up with her dad in the café.
'Hello love do you want a coffee'? he asked her,
'Yes please dad', she replied and sat down at the table with him.
Laura dried the tears from her eyes.
'I've just spoken to Ross's parents they will be here this afternoon to,
see him' she told her dad.
Charlie placed the cup of coffee in front of her.
I don't know what were going to do dad' she said to him'
'I know' replied Charlie, 'it's not going to be easy for you love but,
you're not on your own remember that were all here for you'.
'I know dad' she replied.
What was going to happen to them now and little James?
They could manage financially with her job.
She finished her coffee.
Then they both headed back the wards to see Ross.
'I've let your mum and dad know the news'
'I'm so sorry Ross' said Laura
'You go home you need to get some rest, 'replied Ross.
What Ross was really trying to say was he wanted to be alone.
Reluctantly Laura got up from the chair and turned to her dad. '
Come on love' said Charlie' let's take you home.
She leaned over and kissed Ross on the forehead,
I'll see you tomorrow she told him.
Charlie took her arm as they walked to the car Laura was in a state of,
shook.
"What are we going to do dad?' again she asked him.
'Why did this have to happen to us?'

'I know it's hard for you love he replied.
But we have to take one day at a time.
There is nothing else we can do' he told her.
They pulled up at Angie's house to pick up James and take,
him home.
'Hello Laura, Charlie' said Angie as she answered the door.
'Come in' James came running up to his mum.
She bent down and gave him a kiss.
Have you had a nice time in the park with Auntie Angie' she said to,
him 'Yes mummy' James said excited.
Laura told Angie all about Ross.
  She thanked her for all she had done for them looking after James,
"what would I have done without you" She said.
"Don't be silly" Angie replied.
'You've got enough to cope with'.
'You know where I am if you need me to look after James anytime if,
there's anything else I can do just let me know'.
'Keep me updated' she told Laura with that they said their goodbyes.
  Laura turned the key in the door.
 She was wondering what life had in store for them now.
  After their evening meal Charlie tucked James in to bed.
  And read him a story.
  James is settled for the night' said Charlie.
"Thanks dad what would I do without you and Ross's parents?'
 Laura burst in to tears; Charlie put his arms around her,
  "I know love' he said.
 "I told you it's not going to be easy for you" he said,
 "But we are all here to help in any way we can.'
  'I wonder what James thinks about it all bless him' said Laura.
 'I know he's not old enough to understand everything.
 But it does affect him as well' Laura said to her dad.
    Laura tossed and turned all night praying for strength to help her,
through each day to come.

She fell into a deep sleep and dreamt about her mother.

She could feel her watching over her, smiling as if she was,
comforting her.

The nurse walked in the room with the drug chart,

She also had a small container in her hand.

"Good morning Mr. Portland' I have your medication here'.
She informed him.

Ross wasn't thinking about what she had just said.

"Are you alright?' asked the other nurse.

What a stupid question to ask was I alright, thought Ross.

Of course he wasn't alright he was in that much pain and he'd just lost,
his golfing career.

His life was never going to be the same.

Ross realized she was waiting for an answer.

'Ok I suppose' he replied in a droll voice.

Well you'll feel better when you've had you tablets replied the nurse,
is that what she thinks thought Ross.

The nurses double checked his details with him from his,

wrist band, and against the chart and dosage of medication,

to be given to Ross.

Both the nurses signed the drug chart.

His arm was in a support sling and he found it difficult to help,
himself up the bed.

Every time he took a deep breath his ribs hurt him.

She placed the tablets on the bedside table.

'Here let me help you' said the other nurse to him.

With the nurses assistance he settled in a more comfortable position.

She poured a glass of water for him and waited whilst he took his,
tablets then left the room.

"Breakfast' Mr. Portland said the hostess lady walking in to the room,
with a tray in her hand.

'I'm not feeling that hungry' Ross said to her as she put the,
tray on the table in front of him.

Ross gave her a half hearted smile.

'You have to eat something to keep up your energy',
She commented.
Energy what did she think he was going to do that day.
Run a bloody marathon.
Where's she coming from thought Ross?
"Here's some tea and toast would you like anything else'.
"No thank you" said Ross all he wanted was her to leave,
the room.
'See you later' she said to Ross as she walked out the door.
'Don't bother' he thought.
The morning dragged on and Ross was fed up with the,
Nurse coming in and out of the room with more instructions.
What with medication and checking up on him all the time.
All he wanted was to be left alone,
He was watching the clock every hour and hoping that he wouldn't,
have many visitors.
He wanted the time to himself.
He wasn't in the mode for more advice.
Just then a head peaked around the door and in came a bubbly young,
lady.
Hello Mr. Portland I'm Jasmine your physiotherapist.
How are you feeling this morning?
Tired said Ross.
'Well we need to get you moving out that bed' she told to him.
I need to go through some exercise to strengthen your arm.'
Now the bandages are taken down you can proceed with them.
In the mean time I will leave you a leaflet for you to look at.
Simple as that he thought it's alright for her.
She hasn't got to put up with this.
Exercise was the last thing on his mind.
'Thank you' he said, but couldn't wait for her to leave the room.
'I'll see you later and if you have any question to ask,
I will try and answer them' she said and off she went.

Bloody exercises Ross said to himself.

What does she think I can do?

Ross was finding it awkward trying to do things with his, arm in a sling.

Every time he moved his ribs hurt him, it took his breath, away for a few seconds.

His leg was painful from the deep cuts, and sore from the, skin graft.

The pain relief hardly touched it sometimes.

He thought to himself what a mess he was in.

And she wants me to do physiotherapy she must be joking thought, Ross.

The physiotherapist returned.

'Told you I would be back 'she said to Ross.

'Yes you did 'Replied Ross with a sunken feeling.

'You see you won't get of lightly with me' she joked to Ross.

Now let's get you out of this bed and in to the bathroom so you can, freshen up' she said to him.

'Well' I can't manage on my own' commented Ross.

I'll buzz for the nurse to come and give us a hand Replied Jasmine.

Ross didn't reply, all he could think of was a nurse having to wash, him.

It took a lot of effete in everything he did.

When everything was done he was assisted to the chair,

'Do you good to sit out for a little while, a change of position, for your bottom' said the nurse.

Bottom anyone would think she was talking to a baby.

Ross thought.

After lunch Ross was assisted back on the bed.

The morning events had tired him, and the pain was kicking, in from his shoulder.

All Ross wanted to do was have his medication then sleep.

Knowing it would soon be visiting time.

Laura poked her head round the door.

'Look who I've brought to see you' she told him James?

The nurse said it was ok for him to come and visit you.

Look James, daddy's got a poorly arm'

Poorly arm thought Ross is that what she calls it?

"Show daddy the elephant we found in his bag,"

"And thanks for the perfume" she said

James pushed the elephant under Ross's nose.

"Hey don't do that" Laura said to him.

James began to sulk 'sorry daddy' he said then carried on,

to say 'look daddy when you wind it up his ears flap just like a real,
elephant and he moves his legs', James told him.

Ross didn't answer him he just looked at him.

James started to grizzle.

Laura sat him on the bed with the toy.

Ross put on a brave face for Laura.

He watched James's every move and asked how they were getting on.

"Has mum been to help out "asked Ross?

Everyone's been great replied Laura.

'I can't thank your mum, dad and sister enough they have been,
wonderful giving us all the support they can.

Josie's taken James out so I could get some rest.

'My boss has given me as much time off as I need.

Dad's been looking after the garden.

So you won't have to worry about cutting the lawns.'

What had she just said?

"Sorry Ross I wasn't thinking' said Laura close to tears.

Ross was getting anxious he didn't want to hear about the bloody,
Lawns.

How was he going to manage the lawn mower?

Laura lifted James off the bed and sat him on the floor.

James was beginning to annoy Ross touching everything around him.

'Leave that alone' said Ross to him, when James went to,
touch the electric bed controls.

'I think it's time you took him home' he said to Laura.

'He's getting tired.

What Ross really meant was he'd had enough of him.

He was full of life running around the room.

Ross just wanted some peace and quiet.

Laura knew he was annoying him.

She picked him up in her arms.

'James say good bye to daddy and you can see him tomorrow' she, said to him.

Laura lifted James up to give Ross a kiss.

"I'll be back to see you later, 'dad will look after James."

"We'll let daddy get some rest. Laura told her son.

'Let's go and see what granddads been up to shall we.

'Wave goodbye to daddy James'.

'I'll see you later' Laura told him as they walked out the door.

Chapter 20

The time came for Ross to be discharged from hospital.
Now you know what I've told you' said Mr. Turner.
'It will take time to heal and you'll have to be patient'.
'You have an appointment to see me in 6 Weeks time.
We'll see how you're getting on then'.
'We have arranged for you to see the physiotherapist.
You have all the instruction regarding wearing your sling brace;
don't forget to take your pain relief regular.
   Ross thanked Mr. Turner and nurses for looking after him.
Laura handed them a thank you card and box of chocolates,
   "Much appreciated" said the sister "now you take care'.
Laura opened the car door.
   Ross settled himself into the seat anxious about the Journey
home.
He found it awkward trying to wear a seat belt with the sling,
supporting his shoulder.
It brought back memories of the car crash.
"You all right Ross' said Laura 'you look a bit pasty".
'I'm ok it's just being in the car brings back flashes of the crash',
   'I know love I'll drive slowly' She replied.
Ross knew he had to put his trust in Laura.
She wasn't Jimmy.
   'By the way he said have you heard from Jimmy'.
'He phoned a couple of times, and I was quizzing him about,
   what really happened' Laura told him.
   He was very quiet on the phone and said he wasn't,
Feeling too good',

She went on to say, 'I can't get it out of my head,
that he was to blame for all of this'.
'I don't think he realizes what he's done to us.
How does he think we're going to manage'?
Laura was annoyed with her remarks, and realized she,
shouldn't have said that.
What was she thinking of while Ross was still in a delicate state?
Ross just stared out the car window.
She was right, how were they going to manage.
He couldn't do anything in his condition.
All Ross was thinking about, he was going to be more.
of a burden to her.

The weeks flew by for Laura rushing from work to picking,
James up from nursery, then trying to help Ross as much as,
she could.
Phillip came to take him to physiotherapy.
He was assisted by Jasmine the therapist movements,
to help to strengthen his arm.
He would have to support his shoulder with a sling brace,
He had also lost the use of his hand, his injuries would take time to,
heal inside, and nothing was going to be easy for Ross.
He would no longer be able to grip a golf club.
Mary came over to help in the house and with James.
Laura was grateful for all she did for them.
Ross was getting more frustrated and depressed.
The days dragged by and he was limited to what he could,
do for himself and Laura.
He struggled getting dressed trying to button his shirt, he found it,
difficult only having the use of one hand.
He found it more awkward trying to do the simplest things.
Some days he just gave up.
There where times he found the pain was unbearable.
Ross tried to keep on top of it all with his pain relief.
Charlie came round to help in the garden in the week.
Ross hadn't heard from Jimmy that frustrated him more.
Considering they had been such good friends.
Jimmy was at the garage collecting his new car.

When he turned around he saw one of Ross's friends.

"Hello Jimmy how are you doing' he asked him.

I've been out of town I heard about the crash what happened'.

Jimmy froze for a moment before answering.

"I swerved to miss   a van he said and ran into a tree."

'What about your friend' he asked.

"Ross took the full force of the crash, I escaped with few injuries."

Some bruised ribs, cuts to my face and hands.

"Guess I was the lucky one Ross has life changing Injuries' replied Jimmy.

I heard he was in a bad way, and they have a little boy his wife must be worried to death. His friend commented.

Jimmy's mind was in turmoil all those questions.

He hadn't thought of anything but being responsible for the accident.

"I know it's going be hard for him' replied Jimmy.

Did he really know how hard it was going to be for all of them?

"When you see him Jimmy send him my regards and tell him,

I'll be in touch'.

"I've just brought a new house in the village" said his friend.

He tapped Jimmy on the shoulder 'take care see you around'.

'Thanks said Jimmy' I'll pass the message on'.

Jimmy hadn't been in touch with Ross since the accident.

He couldn't face him all those questions he'd have to answer.

What if Ross found out Jimmy and Josie had been seeing each other all this time, neither of them had mentioned it to him or the family.

The police was already talking off dangerous driving.

What with that and the insurance company onto him regarding damages he couldn't think straight.

He knew everyone was blaming him for the crash.

Then he did cause the crash, he was the one behind the wheel.

Josie knew if it came out she had been seeing Jimmy it would,

Set off fireworks all round.

Ross would be angry about it all.

Also what about her parents, Laura, and Charlie.

That would not go down very well with any off them.

But she loved Jimmy and he loved Josie.

They never meant any of it to happen to them both.

Josie was caught between the two.

She couldn't talk to Ross about it.

She remembered what Ross would say to her, 'pity the woman he, marries'.

The last thing he wanted was his sister to be caught up with someone, like Jimmy.

She hated lying to them all, but ached for Jimmy.

Ross was watching James at meal time trying to get the food from his, plate on his fork.

'Hey don't throw your food on the floor 'he snapped.

James burst into tears.

Laura could see Ross was frustrated.

She walked over to James and gave him a cuddle.

'Daddy didn't mean it' she said to him, and sat next to him.

She turned to Ross, 'don't take it out on him' she said.

'I know you get frustrated because you can't do what you want to and, you don't like having to ask everyone to do things for you'.

'James doesn't deserve to be shouted at'.

Ross got up and walked out the kitchen.

He knew she was right he felt irritable and mad with himself for, getting cross with James.

All the physiotherapy he had been having would not bring back the, grip in his hand.

He hated having to wear the brace sling day in day out.

He was tired of having to focus on day to day adjustments in his life, He needed to get out of the house.

As he walked around the garden his mind was going round in circles.

'I can't live like this' he said to himself and sat down under the tree, and broke down in tears.

Laura cleared away the dishes and cleaned up after James.

After changing James clothes she sorted out the washing Life was, tough for her juggling work and a family.

There wasn't much time for herself.

Mr Mailing pulled up to the big gates.

He got out of his car and walked over to the intercom.

Pressed the button, 'Is Mr Portland available to speak to' he said when, Laura answered.

'And you are' replied Laura.

'Oh sorry' Mr Mailing I'm from the insurance company regarding his, car accident.

'I'll let you in' Replied Laura.

Laura pressed the button to open the gates.

Mr. Mailing drove his car up to the front door.

Laura stood there waiting for him.

Laura noticed as he got out the car he was a very good looking young, man.

'Is it Mrs. Portland', he asked Laura?

'Yes, 'you had better come in' She replied 'I'll just get my husband, he's in the garden'.

Ross had seen the man coming up the drive.

Laura went into the garden 'Ross there's a Mr.Mailing from the, Accident and Insurance Company he would like to talk to you', said Laura.

'Oh I wondered who that was coming up the drive' commented Ross.

He knew he'd have to talk to him sooner or later about the accident.

"I'll, be there in a minute" Ross told her.

He wasn't looking forward to being reminded of it all.

But he needed to especially when it came to finance's.

'Take a seat in the conservatory 'said Laura to him.

My husband will be with you in a moment.

'Would you like a coffee' Laura asked Mr. Mailing?

'That would be nice one sugar and little milk '.

He replied.

Just then Ross walked in Mr. Mailing got up and introduced, himself, to Ross then sat down again.

'Coffee Ross' Laura asked, 'yes please' was the reply.

Laura headed to the kitchen to make the coffee.

Laura made the cups of coffee and took them in to the conservatory.

She put them on the table, turned around looked at Ross and said 'I will leave you men to talk'.

Then she made her way back to the kitchen.

An hour had passed by.

Laura decided to go and collect the coffee cups also to see how the, conversation was going.

She could see Ross was getting edgy all the time answering questions.

As she was about to leave, she turned to speak to Mr. Mailing.

'Could we continue this another time' she said

'I think my husband is getting tired'.

'Very well, but I do have to get all the facts to sort out a settlement for, your injuries' he replied.

Settlement thought Ross however much it was going to be it was, never enough for what quality of life he would have to live with.

Chapter 21

Ross took an afternoon nap.

On waking he heard the sound of the lawn mower.

It should be me cutting the lawn he thought.

He knew he had to get up and face Charlie although he didn't feel like, it.

Not after the visit from Mr. Mailing the day before.

He didn't want to go through all the rigmarole with Charlie.

Laura had warned her dad about the insurance man questioning, Ross and how it had frustrated him.

She did not want him quizzed again about it.

She knew Ross was tired of it all and wanted him to be left alone.

Charlie didn't say anything to him that day.

He just hoped it would all soon be sorted out.

The weeks went by.

Ross wondered when he would hear from the insurance company, regarding payment for the accident.

Ross looked out the window he could see the post man struggling to, push the letters in the mail box.

He decided to walk to the gate and collect them.

He wanted to know if there was any update from, Mr. Mailings visit.

Laura came in from the garden went into the kitchen to put the kettle, on to make them all a drink.

She picked up a cup, tapped on the window,

Coffee dad' she said to him, holding up the cup.

Charlie nodded yes; she made them all a coffee.

Charlie had finished edging the lawns and was ready for a drink.

'Phew it's warm out there today love' he said to Laura.

'Sit down dad and have your coffee, unless you want a, Cold drink' she replied.

'No this is ok' he told her.

Ross joined them both at the kitchen table.

'Anything interesting in the mail today', Laura said to Ross.

'No only bills' He commented.

He took a seat next to Charlie.

'Thanks for cutting the lawns' he said to him.

'I do appreciate what you do'.

Charlie was wondering did he really appreciate what everyone was, doing for him.

He knew it had not been easy for Ross.

But it was as though everyone was running around doing, their best.

While he was wallowing in self pity some of the time.

Did he know what Laura had to put up with?

What with her working all week, and looking after James, then coming home to Ross.

Putting up with his mood swings.

Charlie could see it was taking its toll on her.

The next morning Ross decided to take a walk down the lane.

He saw the for sale sign, had been taken down outside the, neighbouring house.

He wondered who had brought it.

Looks like we will have new neighbour's he thought.

But then he didn't see much of them anyway.

It was a quiet area everyone pretty much kept themselves to, themselves.

Laura spoke to them more than he did.

She often walked down the lane with James.

They would put their hand up to her when she drove by.

Charlie had been back the next day to cut down some trees.

He was just about to get in his car when Laura's car pulled, in the drive.

Charlie stood there waiting to see how she was.

As Laura got out of the car she reached into the back to lift a box, from off the seat.

 Charlie went up to her 'here love let me take that for you he 'said 'It's alright dad I've got it she replied'.

 'You're home early is everything alright'? Charlie commented.

 'Yes I managed to get off earlier today'.

 'So I stopped off to do the shopping' she replied.

'Josie picking James up from nursery and taken him back to her, parents for the weekend'.

'They can have some time with their grandson'

She said to her dad.

 Ross parent loved having James.

 Josie liked to take him to the park to feed the ducks.

 'That good of them it will give you a rest 'said Charlie.

'Well I'll be off you look after yourself '.

'I've got a date' he said to her.

'A date who with' she said with a suspicious look on her face.

'Ah got you going there young lady' commented Charlie.

'The hairdresser I'm going to have my ears lowered' he replied.

 Laura laughed.

 'You had me going for a moment' she replied.

'Well at least it brought a smile to your face' said Charlie.

'I'll speak to you another day look after yourself'.

'I will dad' She replied.

Charlie said his goodbyes to them both and was on his way.

Laura was cooking the evening meal.

 "What have you been up to today Ross" she asked.

 Not much although he never was up to much.

'Not heard from any one then, no phone calls'.

 Laura said to him.

'No' replied Ross

 'Who would bother phoning me anyway' He commented.

 Laura knew Ross was getting more depressed.

Whilst they were having their evening meal Laura knew she had to, tackle a difficult subject.

She placed her knife and fork on the plate and looked at Ross.

'Ross she said 'I was talking to my friend at the courts the other day'.

'She was telling me about a good therapist who helps people in, difficult times to try and find way to approach problems and improve things'.

'She sounds very interesting' 'It may help you to see someone think, about it.'

Ross looked at Laura was he hearing right.

What was she talking about how did she know how he felt.

Had she any idea how this had affected him.

His life was not the same and never would be again.

He just stared at her.

Laura knew she'd said the wrong thing.

Sorry Ross I wasn't thinking let's leave it.

'To right' he said and stormed out of the kitchen.

We'll that went down well she thought to herself,

I give up.

Ross lay in bed thinking about the accident.

No news about the compensation.

He hadn't heard from Jimmy for a while and knew he was avoiding, him.

If it wasn't for him arguing in the car with him that day it wouldn't, have happened,

He tossed and turned all night thinking of nothing else.

Feeling as though his head was going to burst and sweating.

He jumped out of bed, Laura woke up startled.

"What's the matter Ross"? She asked.

"Go back to sleep Laura, I'm just going down for a drink.

"He said to her.

A drink, more like a bottle full thought Laura.

She laid her head back down on the pillow thinking how much more, could she take.

It was as hard for her what with his mood swings and snapping at, James.

He was drinking more.

Is this it she thought to herself?

Was this what her life was going to be like from here on?

She dozed off waking late.

Laura was rushing around tidying the house.

Then she pegged the washing on the line.

James was at his grandparents.

She was going to meet her friend Maggie for a coffee in town.

They hadn't met up for some time.

What with everything that had happened.

Laura phoned Maggie to tell her she would be a little late, arriving.

'That ok Laura' Maggie replied.

'I have some shopping to do so I'll do that first'.

Laura put her mobile phone in her handbag.

"Who's that" said Ross.

"Oh Maggie" came the reply.

"I'm meeting her for coffee I haven't seen her for a while."

"I thought has your mum's got James for the weekend.

I'd catch up with her.

'That ok with you Ross".

"Unless there was something you wanted to do."

She commented.

"No Laura you go and have a coffee with your friend.

"Don't worry about me here on my own after all I'm only your, husband'.

'That's not fair Ross' Laura snapped back.

I've hardly seen my friends, what with working,

Coming home doing all I can around the house.

"Whilst Looking after James, surely you don't begrudge me having, coffee with my friend'.

"You say that as though I don't care."

"I've bent over backwards to help and support you"

"Do you not realize it's been hard for me too?"
"It doesn't only affect you'
"It's like we've all been treading on egg shells"
'Giving you time to come to terms with what happened."
"All you do is feel sorry for yourself.'
  Laura stopped and released what she had said.
 How could she speak to him like that, what was she thinking of.
"So sorry Ross I didn't mean to say that" she told him.
  But she knew it was right in what she had just said.
   Laura put on her coat and rushed out the front door the tears,
falling down her face.
 Regretting every word she had said to him.
 Maybe she should have said them before instead of bottling it all up,
it would have cleared the air before now.
 What was happening to them both?

Chapter 22

Laura pulled into the car park and found a space in the,
corner near a hedge.
She freshened up her makeup and tidied her hair.
She didn't want Maggie to see she'd been crying?
Maggie was sitting at a table near the window and saw,
Laura come rushing through the door.
"Hello Maggie' she said 'sorry I'm late, it's lovely to see you."
Maggie put her arm around her and gave her a hug.
"Have you been waiting long?"Laura asked.
"No I've only been here five minutes' she replied.
Laura sat down beside her.
'It's been a while since I saw you, what would you like to drink",
asked Maggie.
"Just coffee she replied.
Maggie beckoned to the waiter and ordered two Coffees'.
"He's not bad looking she said to Laura, in fact he's quite a dish,''
commented Maggie.
Laura blushed "Maggie's, he's old enough to be your Son" she told,
her.
'Well there's no harm in looking and he's got a cute bottom."
'It keeps you feeling young" said Maggie.
'Yes" replied Laura solemnly.
Where had all the years gone she thought, how she missed,
that part.
What it would be like to be young again.
Not having a care in the world.
'Laura what's up" said Maggie.
'You look as though you've been crying."
'How are things at home if you don't mind me asking' questioned,
Maggie.
Laura held back the tears.

'Oh Maggie I don't know what to do anymore'.
  She poured her heart out to her.
  Maggie had always been a good listener and took in all,
  what Laura was saying to her?
  'What do you want Laura" Maggie said to her.
  'You have to think of James also, it can't be easy for you all."
  "Can you get Ross's friend to talk to him."
  That's all very well" Laura said.
"Jimmy has never been in touch with Ross since the accident."
  I know it's not been easy for Ross living with his condition'.
  Ross is so mixed up with his emotions; I don't think he realizes,
  he's losing us" Commented Laura.
  Have you thought that maybe Jimmy blames himself and can't face,
Ross' said Maggie?
'He was driving the car' replied Laura.
  "I know but think of how he feels; he will never get away from what,
happened that night'.
'Don't get me wrong Laura; I'm not making excuses for him' Maggie,
told her.
'It doesn't excuse him for not getting in touch with Ross'.
'After all they were the best of friends'.
"One minute you have everything in life."
"Then it's snatched away from you like a blink of an eye,"
  Said Laura.
  'It must be taking its toll on your marriage' said Maggie to her.
"Why don't you contact Jimmy and see what he has to say,
  about it all."
  Laura listened with intense to what Maggie had said to her.
  Laura went on to say 'then there's the insurance it's taking,
  such a long time to sort out,"
    "Sorry Maggie I've gone on and on about it."
"I haven't asked what you've been up to how selfish of me'.
    "Well if you want to know I've been busy buying a place in,
  Spain' Maggie told her.

"Really, Spain wow that great for you how exciting'.

"When are you going out there?' asked Laura.

"In three weeks time, why don't you and James come with me?

'It would do you both the world of good' Maggie told her.

"Thanks that sound very nice I'll think about it' replied Laura.

Well don't take too long thinking about it' commented Maggie.

Laura looked down at her watch.

"Gosh is that the time I have to go' she said.

'Thanks Maggie for listening to me you're a good friend."

'That's what I'm here for Laura, and don't you forget young lady,' Maggie told her.

'Now let me pay for the coffee I want to get that dashing waiter's, attention again."

Laura laughed "Maggie really."

"See that brought a smile to your face" said Maggie. "We will have, to come here again'.

"Now don't forget', said Maggie 'three weeks time Spain.

The offers open so let me know".

She gave Maggie a hug.

'It's been so lovely catching up I'll phone you.'

'Make sure you do' replied Maggie'

'Think about what I said about Spain seriously'.

'I would love you to come'.

'I will' replied Laura, bye then and take care'.

Laura walked to the car.

She was dreading going home wondering what mood Ross would be, in.

But she was thinking all the way home what Maggie had said to her about Jimmy.

Maybe she should talk to him and find out why he was avoiding Ross.

Laura opened the front door.

"Ross I'm home" she shouted but there was no reply.

Where could he be she thought, maybe he's in the garden.

She walked into the garden and saw him sitting in the sun house.

"Hello" said Ross "did you have a nice time with Maggie."

"Yes" she replied.

She knew she had to pick the right moment to approach,

Ross about getting in touch with Jimmy.

She sat there asking him about his day.

She told him about Maggie's place in Spain, now she had his attention, she would approach the subject.

"Ross' she said 'Maggie was asking if Jimmy had been in touch."

"I told her you hadn't heard from him."

"Why don't you phone and arrange for him to come over and talk'.

"Maybe it's time you got things out in the open."

You both need to move on.

Ross was angry that Laura should even suggest such a thing,

"Why the bloody hell should I call him', he said to her.

"He's not even bothered to phone me himself."

"You must be joking, don't you realize what he's done'.

"He's ruined my life and career".

"If you think for one minute I'm going to be the first to pick up, the phone and call him"

"He can get lost as far as I'm concerned".

"As for you Laura, I'm surprised you would even think of such a thing, what's the matter with you don't you care."

'Of course I care more than you think "Replied Laura.

"I just thought it would be good to talk to Jimmy that's all'.

'Forget it I wish I had never mentioned it',

With that Laura walked off in to the kitchen to prepare a meal.

Charlie phoned that evening and Laura told him what had happened.

What am I to do dad she said.

I can't go on much longer I've tried.

She broke down in tears.

Charlie wished he was there to hug her and tell her everything would, be alright.

But knew it wouldn't unless Ross got some help.

"Look love I'll come over Monday whilst you're at work and talk to, him.
'See if I can get him to go and talk to someone".
I've tried that dad my friend gave me a number of a Psychologist, whom she saw and said was very good'.
 'But he's adamant he won't talk to anyone' Replied Laura.
"Have you talked to your doctor maybe you should make an, appointment."
 "There are people out there that understand what you're going through. You need to look after yourself' Commented Charlie.
 Laura knew her dad wouldn't pull any punches with Ross.
 He could see it was hurting his daughter and knew if he didn't speak to Ross.
 Their marriage was in jeopardy, also what about little James.

Ross wandered in to the kitchen.
"By the way Laura, Josie's calling in tonight.'
'She is bringing something round for James."Ross told her.
 "Well I know she had been away the other weekend for a few days, your Mum was telling me' Laura told him.
'Well she didn't say anything to me when she picked James up, the other day' said Ross 'Oh well never mind replied Laura.
 Just then the intercom buzzer went.
"I'll go that could be her now', Laura opened the gates.
 Josie drove up to the front door, as Laura opened the door.
Josie stood there with a bag full of items for James.
 Come in Josie we've just been talking about you." Laura said.
 "Oh really', anything interesting "replied Josie.
 "Ross chipped in I was just telling Laura you were calling,
 That's all".
"Unless you have something to tell us" Commented Laura.
 Josie blushed did they know she had been away with Jimmy.
"No'? Should there be' she quickly changed the subject.

Let's take your coat Josie, now what can I get you to drink' Laura, asked.

'Coffee would be fine as I'm driving' said Josie.

"Ross is in the lounge go in and take a seat"

With that Laura went off to the kitchen to make the coffee.

Josie settled in the chair.

"Did you have a nice break the other weekend then' asked Ross.

"Yes relaxing."Josie commented.

"Mum told Laura you went to Cornwall."

"Did you go with anyone or by yourself' said Ross inquisitively.

"I took a friend "Josie replied.

Not letting on it was Jimmy she'd been with.

Ross didn't say anything else.

"I brought James a toy and some books."

"That was nice of you "replied Ross.

Laura placed the coffee on the table.

"Well did you have a nice time away Laura said to Josie?

"Lovely came the reply.

"I was ready for a break it's been that busy at the shop."

"It was nice to get away commented Josie.

Not giving too much information away.

"I heard you telling Ross you had been with a friend."

"Yes" she replied, but quickly changed the subject.

She went on to tell them about the toy and other items she had, brought James.

"That's very nice of you' said Laura 'but you shouldn't spoil him."

Josie put down the coffee cup and looked at Ross.

He looked drawn in the face and had lost the sparkle in his eyes.

"What have you been up to then Ross's "she said to him.

"Nothing much" Ross replied.

That was nothing new thought Josie.

Laura told her all about the insurance man coming to talk to Ross, about the accident.

"He came to see Ross about compensation."

"I'm surprised at Jimmy "commented Laura.

"All those years they have been friends then this happens."

"He hasn't got the decency to get in touch."

"And all this is his fault."

Her voice was angry 'how can someone do that to you?

I think I'll phone him and find out why he has been avoiding Ross."

Ross joined in the conversation 'don't bother leave it he's, not worth it."

"I don't know if I'd want him in the house'.

Josie felt the tension rise in her body the redness glow of her cheeks.

She couldn't let on it was Jimmy she had been seeing.

What would that do to Ross and her family?

Knowing she had been away with him to Cornwall.

Keeping it a secret from them all the time.

"Well I'd better go, got to open up the shop early for a delivery", she told them both.

"It's was nice of you to call round', said Laura.

"And thank you for the gifts for James."

"That's ok we'll catch up in the week' she replied.

Then Josie put her coat on and was on her way.

Laura closed the door and went back into the lounge.

"Josie didn't stay long' she said to Ross.

"Well perhaps she's tired she did say she had been busy in the shop', said Ross.

"Strange though not like her to dash off like that."

"I can't help but think there's more to it than she's letting on" said, Laura.

"What makes you say that' asked Ross.

I noticed how agitated she got when you kept going on about Jimmy.

Did you see how she coloured up when you ask her if she had been, away on her own" Commented Laura

Ross wasn't really bothered.

All he could think of was Jimmy after Laura had mentioned him to, Josie.

It niggled away at him like an Itch he couldn't scratch.

Chapter 23

Laura settled down for the night.

Not mentioning to Ross about the conversation between her and her, dad.

Knowing it wouldn't go down very well with Ross.

Laura stirred early in the morning took a shower then dressed.

She got James his breakfast then dressed him ready for nursery.

James wasn't in any mood to put his coat on.

Ross grabbed the coat from Laura.

"Here let me do that" he said while you're getting your ready.

"Daddy "James shouted excitedly jumping up and down.

"Come on son" said Ross" let's get your coat on stop messing, about your mum's got to go to work'.

Ross struggled to get James arm in the coat with only having, the use of one arm himself.

James tried to button the coat up.

'Leave it' said Ross to him in a sharp tone 'mummy's got to get to, work'.

Laura opened the car door and strapped James in his car seat.

"Don't forget your mum's picking James up from nursery she shouted, to Ross,"

"OK was his reply.

"By then see you tonight "Replied Laura.

Laura waved goodbye as she pulled out the driveway.

Ross walked into the kitchen and attempted to fill the dishwasher.

Then he decided to read the daily paper.

The intercom buzzed, he wondered who it could be this early in the, morning.

He answered the intercom, 'It's me' said Charlie to him.

He opened the gates he was surprised to see Charlie.

"Come in Charlie I wasn't expecting you this early is everything, alright".

'Well you tell me' said Charlie; I've come to talk".

"Why's that" asked Ross with a curious look on his face.

"I know you don't want me to interfere but I'm worried about Laura" said Charlie'

"She's had to cope with a lot lately.

'I know it's not your fault what happened."

Charlie went on laying down a few facts and was trying to,

get Ross to realize it was not just him it was affecting.

It was also Laura and James.

"Maybe you need to think about what help you could get out there."

"What like therapy"? said Ross rather angrily.

"Do you think I don't know what you're suggesting a shrink,

"shouted Ross at him.

"No said Charlie, but you need to talk to someone,

to help you move forward.

Charlie couldn't contain his anger any longer.

"We've all tried to help now it's time you helped yourself".

"Not just for you but for your family can't you see it's not fair on, Laura ".

"She supported you, and it's time you gave something back."

Charlie got up and walked to the door.

"I don't want to fall out with you Ross ".

"Think about it for all your sakes."

"We all mean well and know it's not been easy for you".

"Losing your career and coping with your injuries.

"Maybe it will help you more than you think."

Charlie had said enough.

"How do you know what I think replied Ross?

"In fact I think you'd better go."

"Ok Ross' replied Charlie' if that's how you want to be.

'I'm not falling out with you I'll be on my way'.

Before Charlie walked out the door he turned to Ross and said to him.

'Think about what I said Ross, the last thing I would want to,
see is your marriage to break up.'
Charlie left with mixed feelings.
Hoping Ross would come to his senses and get some help.

Ross walked back to the kitchen.
Picking up the glass from the table he grabbed a bottle of whisky,
and poured himself a drink.
He walked around the room talking to himself.
'How does anyone know what I want?
After all he didn't know what he wanted himself.
'Coming here and telling me what to do and not do'.
'What's it got to do with Charlie or anyone else for that matter'?
'I bet Laura put him up to this.'
They should all mind their own business.
How dare he come and preach to me about family life.
Ross had become callous and self-obsessed.
Cursing what Charlie had just said to him.
 The scenes from the accident were going round and round,
 in his head.
What am I going to do he questioned himself?
His mind was racing with different thoughts.
He hated himself for feeling the way he did.
It was as if everything was spiraling out of control.
How could he go on like this?
There had to be something more to life.
 He took a swig of whisky, but Ross knew the answer wasn't,
 from a bottle.
 People would come and go but Ross didn't feel their presence some,
times.
The doctors and physiotherapist had given all the help they could.
It was all down to him now.
He slumped down in the chair so tired and dozed off.

When Ross woke he was angry with himself,

How could he have spoken to Charlie like that after all he had done to, help them?

Where would he have been without all his help in the garden and, around the house?

He was also angry with Jimmy for not getting in touch with him.

It was as if they had never known each other.

That was no way to treat his best friend Ross thought.

Things would have been different if he hadn't argued in the car, that day with Jimmy about his driving.

He wouldn't have been in the situation he was now.

They would still be on the golf tours.

He kicked the door in his frustration.

Walked over to the kitchen table sat down, clasping his head in his, hand.

The thought of losing Laura and James went through his mind.

That's what could happen if he carried on this way.

He couldn't see a way out of it all.

His mind was lost in some dark place.

Maybe he did need some help.

He didn't want to admit it to himself.

Ross put his coat on and walked down the lane.

The leaves on the trees were turning their autumn colour.

He loved the changes it was a spectacular display of gold and bronze, mixed with the yellows and greens.

It was such a quiet area where they lived they had very little traffic.

Which he liked that was one of the reason he bought the house.

Whilst out walking the thought crossed his mind what Laura had said, about Josie.

Laura's firm had just won a court case,
She decided to join some of her work colleagues to celebrate at the, local wine bar.
They found a quiet corner near the fire place.
She was just going to sit down at the table, when she heard Maggie's, voice.
She peered around the corner to see the young waiter taking an order, for a drink.
"Hello Maggie what are you doing here or need I ask" she said, laughing.
Maggie got up and gave her a hug.
"Well you know darling' she said' you have to keep your spirits up, some times.
'Anyway what are you doing here may I ask," commented Maggie.
"Oh we've just won a big court case, so we all came to celebrate".
"Lucky you, and how's Ross."
   "No different if anything it's getting worse."
"I've tried to talk to him about getting some help".
"But it's just falling on deaf ears".
"Maybe we need some time apart "Commented Laura.
   "Well said Maggie we can arrange that".
"Why don't you take some time off work and come with me to my, apartment in Spain' said Maggie.
Oh I don't know' Laura said 'what would Ross say'.
Now it was Maggie's turn to lay the law down.
   'Look Laura you need to come first for a change".
"James would love the beach, and you could have some quality time, with him', Maggie went on,
"It would be an adventure for him."
"I may just do that "Laura replied.
"You deserve a break Commented Maggie.
"Anyway I don't want to take you away from your work colleague's, think about it."
"Give me a call and let me know' said Maggie.
"Ok I will, replied Laura giving Maggie a hug.

Laura joined her colleagues for a drink.
She knew it would have to be a quick soft drink non alcoholic.
She had to collect James from nursery.

Laura pulled up in the drive thinking about what Maggie had said.

In fact that was the only thing going through her mind all the way, home.

She needed to get away to have some time to herself to think.

She would wait a few days before mentioning it to Ross.

She helped James out the car seat.

'Let's see what daddy's been up to' she said to him

"James ran to the door trying to reach the handle".

"Come here young man, shouted Laura 'you need to grow a bit".

Laura opened the door.

James rushed into the hall slinging his coat on the floor.

Ross walked up to him 'pick that coat up 'he said in a sharp voice', 'It doesn't go on the floor let's put it on coat hook".

James just tossed the coat to Ross.

He ran into the kitchen, waiting for a drink.

Ross gave Laura a peck on the cheek.

"Have you had a good day? He asked.

"Yes' she replied.

"Have you' She commented to Ross'

Knowing her dad had been to see him.

"Not bad "He replied.

"What answer would she have expected from him?

She went on to say 'in fact I've had a really good day'.

'We won our court case today'

'Some of us decided to go to the local wine for a drink, to celebrate."

'Oh and whilst I was there I saw Maggie'.

'Really' Ross replied with a sarcastic tone in his voice.

Laura quickly changed the subject.

"I'll get something for us to eat then James can have a bath and get, ready for bed "She replied.

Laura didn't feel like making a meal after her talk with Maggie.
But knew they all had to eat.

After they had eaten she cleared the table, then she bathed James.
"Story time" she said to James has she tucked him up in bed.
"Does daddy want to read to you tonight?"
Ross wasn't in any mood for reading a bed time story.
"Mummy's better at it than me" Ross replied.
What he really meant was he didn't want to read to his son.

As Laura read to James he soon drifted off to sleep.

Laura settled in the chair

She looked across at Ross.
"Have you had any visitor today?" she asked.
"Yes your dad called round this morning" was his reply.
"Oh did he "Commented Laura.

Laura was not letting on that she knew.

"What did he have to say then"?
"Nothing much Ross grunted.

Ross evaded any question Laura asked.

As she sat there a feeling of despondent came over her.
She thought what do I have to do to get through to him?
Wondering what was going on in his mind.

She could visualize the wheels going round in his head.

Tired of trying to make a conversation Laura decided she would,
have shower.

After her shower she decided to turn in for the night.
"Well I'm off to bed' she said to him' got a busy day tomorrow new,
case to study".

All Ross could reply was 'Ok'.

Laura lay in bed thinking that's it, she thought.

Where going to Spain.
I'll take the offer of Maggie's place in the sun.
James and I need it and deserve it, Sod him.

When Ross comes to bed I'll tell him.
I'm booking the flight tomorrow.

She thumped the pillow.
Settled down and waited in anticipation.

Chapter 24

When she told Ross he didn't seem too worried.

'James would love it on the beach making sand castles.

And paddling in the sea.' she told him,

It was as if he was happy she was going.

He would be on his own.

No dictating from anyone telling him to sort himself out.

The weeks couldn't go by quick enough for Laura.

She was busy shopping and packing the cases.

She brought James a small suit case he could pull along.

Shaped like an elephant to put in the hold on the plane.

He was excited to be going on a plane.

She had organized her work load with the other girls.

They all agreed she needed a break.

Saturday came Maggie was coming to pick up Laura and James.

The cases were packed and ready in the hall.

"Here she is' said Laura to James as Maggie swung the car up to the, drive entrance.

Maggie didn't need to get out of the car and press the button to speak, through the intercom.

Laura had seen her enter the drive on the camera in the house so she, lifted James up to press the button.

He stood at the doorway and watched the gates open.

He was so excited to see Maggie drive her car up to the front door, James jumped up and down.

Maggie had hardly got out of the car before James shouted.

'Auntie Maggie' to her 'were going on a big Airplane'.

'I know' she replied bending down to give him a hug.'

Laura put James car seat in the car and loaded the cases in the boot.

"Give daddy a hug and kiss" she said to James.

Ross bent down and put his arm around him.

"Have a good time "James he said.

Maggie helped him into the car seat then strapped him in.

Laura turned around looked at Ross wishing things were different, and it was him going with them.

Although she was grateful of Maggie's offer.

"Look after yourself" she said to Ross.

"Why wouldn't I" he replied."What harm am I going to get into here, on my own"?.

Laura wasn't sure how to take that comment.

It made her feel guiltier about going.

But she knew she couldn't back out now.

"I'll phone you when we've arrived "she said to him.

He gave her a peck on the cheek.

'Bye all see you when you get back' replied Ross. 'Wave to daddy'.

Laura said to James as Maggie drove out the driveway.

The plane landed on time and James couldn't wait to get off.

"Leave the case James, the young man will bring it for you.

Hold mummy's hand so you don't fall down the steps' she told him.

Laura thanked the young man for helping her.

James stepped on to the tarmac squealing with excitement".

Maggie sorted the cases from the carousel throwing them on the, trolley.

The car was collected from the airport and they were on their way.

When they reached the apartment James could see the beach.

"Look mummy he said"' water', jumping up and down.

'Yes that's the beach we'll go later, once we have unpacked the cases, and had some lunch' his mum told him.

Laura phoned Ross to let them know they had arrived safely.

After lunch they decided it was time to go to the beach.

"Slow down young man said Laura.

James was running along the beach".

He couldn't wait to paddle in the sea.

He laughed as the waves came up to his knees.

He was mesmerized by the water running between his toes.

He squealed when it covered them, jumping up when the, Waves came in.

Then they built sand castles and collect some sea shells.

"Look mummy what I've found' said James 'Sea snells'.

"No its sea shell" said Laura laughing.

"Shall we put them round the sand castle to make it look pretty Auntie, Maggie' James said.

Maggie loved him calling her Auntie it made her feel closer to him.

"Yes young man."She replied.

'Do you want a sea shell' he said to Maggie holding one tightly in his, hand?

"That would be very nice' replied Maggie.

"That will be my special treasure."

"I will have to find a special place to keep it safe', she commented.

Maggie put it in a tissue in her bag.

They all had a great fun splashing around in the sea together.

James was tired from the sea air and settled for the night.

Maggie saw Laura standing on the porch.

"Glass of wine" she said" and a penny for them."

"Yes to the wine and I was just thinking."

If only Ross could have enjoyed the day with James like we have", She commented.

What did he say when you phoned him."

"Nothing much" Replied Laura.

Well let's sit out on the porch and enjoy the wine and moon light', said Maggie.

Maggie didn't want to question her anymore.

She wanted her to enjoy her holiday with James.

The days went by too quickly;

They had all enjoyed their days in the sun and relaxing by the pool at, night time.

All the sea air had done wonders for James.

He had loved his time paddling in the sea and running along, the beach, trying to fly a kite Maggie had brought him.

Only one more day left and they would be flying home.

Home to what thought Laura, was anything going to change.

She was tired of trying to hold everything together.

"I've been thinking" Laura said to Maggie.

Maggie looked puzzled what Laura was about to say.

'I've made up my mind I'm leaving Ross"

"I can't go on like this and it's not fair to James".

"He has been so happy these last few days."

"Are you sure that's what you want" Maggie said.

"I mean."

"It's a big thing bringing up a child on your own and working."

I've had enough time to think about it' and being away this,
week from Ross has made me realize.

There's more to our lives mine and James.

"I will give it a few days before I tell him' said Laura.

"I don't want him to think you had anything to do with my decision".

Maggie looked at Laura she had that determined look,
on her face.

Think about this carefully" Maggie replied to her.

'Oh I have don't you worry' she told her.

Chapter 25

The plane had landed and they were on their way home.
As Maggie pulled in to the drive Mary's car was there.
Laura lifted James out of the car, he ran up to Mary.

"Grandma Grandma" he said running to her
"Oh I've missed you young man "She said to him.
Picking him up and swinging him around in circles.
James was giggling.
Ross gave Laura a hug.

"Did you both have a good time "commented Ross?
James was telling his dad about the big sea and how he made sand,
castles.

They talked about the holiday and looked at photos of James paddling,
in the sea.
"James pointed at the photograph of him with the big sand castle he,
had made and the sea shells around it.

"Sounds as though you had great time without me'
said Ross, looking at Laura.
Laura didn't reply she just smiled back.
What did she expect him to say?
Oh darling how I've missed you.
She knew that wasn't going to happen.
So why did she feel disappointment.

'Well I had better sort out a meal then unpack the cases said, Laura.
Mary sensed the atmosphere in the room.
As she got up to leave she turned to Laura and asked her,
Would you like me to pick James up from nursery on Monday?"
"He can have some tea with his grandma and granddad."
She said as she ran her fingers through James hair.
'I'm sure you and Ross have got some catching up to do'.

"That would be lovely" replied Laura.

'Would you like that' she asked James.

James nodded his head in agreement.

'Why don't you all come over for lunch tomorrow' asked Mary.

'You don't want to be cooking when you've just come back off, holiday'.

'By the looks of it you'll be washing most of the day'.

"Ok that would be nice Laura replied.

"Mary gave James a hug and said goodbye to Ross.

'See you tomorrow' she told them as she got in the car.

She sounded her car horn for James and headed for home.

She felt sad that Ross was not more attentive to Laura.

After all she was a good wife and mother.

Why Couldn't Ross see it had been hard for her too?

Laura loaded the clothes in the washing machine.

After lunch James played in the garden whilst Laura unpacked the, rest of the items in suit cases.

Ross didn't offer to help in any way, he just took himself off in the sun, lounge and read the paper.

The rest of the evening was very quiet for Laura, especially after the, fun and laughter she had been having the past week.

'In you get 'said Laura to James as he scrambled in his car seat.

'Were all off to grandma's for lunch'.

Ross walked round to the passenger side.

Opened the door and sat down in the seat.

'I hope she's in a better mood' he said to Laura.

'Why's that' Laura commented.

'Oh nothing' replied Ross.

Realizing what he had just said he didn't want to explain about the, other day.

Laura was pleased of the company after all, tomorrow she would be, back to work.

James told them all about flying on a big plane and making sand, castles.

Don't forget the sea shell you collected' said his mum.

"Look grandma I brought one for you" said James.
 With that James put his hand in his trouser pocket and handed her a, large Shell.
 "Sorry granddad I could only carry one" he commented.
Phillip laughed, "That's alright my boy I'll share grandma's' then he, gave him a big hug.
 Mary and Phillip loved to spend time with him.
Reading and singing nursery rhymes and going to the park.
He had brought so much joy to them.
 Laura looked at them both saddened by the thought they had no Idea, of what was she had planned.

 Laura was sat at her desk at work wondering when the right time was, to tell Ross,
 She had made up her mind she was leaving him was there ever a right, time.
 Tonight she thought I will tell him tonight and get it over.
 Mary decided to call and see Ross and collect some wellingtons for, James.
She was going to take him to the park after nursery.
 Ross stood at the kitchen window staring out to the garden.
 When his mum pressed the intercom bell it startled him.
 Ross answered and opened the gates to let her in.
 "Hello mum I didn't expect to see you this early."
"Is something the matter' he asked.
 "No I've come to collect James wellingtons were taking him to the, park."
"I forgot them Saturday, are you alright' she asked him
 "I don't know mum why did this happen to me."
"What have I got to look forward to in life?"
 Mary had heard it all before.
 With a sharp tone in her voice she replied.
"Do you think you're the only one suffering Ross."
 "How do you think Laura has coped with it all and bringing up, James"?
 "Also she's been holding her job together".
 "I think you need to give her some credit."

"Some women would have walked away from it all".

"Stop feeling sorry for yourself and think of them for a change."

"It's gone on long enough."

"It may have not been easy for you but you have to look to the future."

'Stop being too proud and get yourself some help'.

Ross was taken aback at his mums words.

It was unexpected of her to talk to him like that.

He stood there with a shocked look on his face.

"May be you're right mum" he said.

Then he told her all about Charlie's visit.

"Have you said anything to Laura?" she asked.

"No' he replied".

"Why not" she commented.

"You know you're going to have to face up to things".

"Sort yourself out it's not fair to Laura and James"

"Why won't you get some help?"

"Swallow your pride for once".

Mary was angry with him.

"You have a lovely wife and son do you want to lose them think about, that."

Ross stood there frozen for a moment.

"What do I do?"

"For a start you talk to your wife."

"We're all here to help you know that Ross".

"I have to go now and collect James'.

'I'll see you later, cheer up love."

With that she gave him a peck on the cheek and said goodbye.

Had she said too much, she though as she drove home.

But it needed to be said; it hurt her to see him like this.

Chapter 26

Laura switched off the computer tidied her desk.

Leaving work early than usual, she slung her coat over her arm.

Said her goodbye to the staff and headed for town.

Tonight was the night she would tell Ross.

Mary was looking after James.

She would have no interruption.

First she was going to meet Maggie for a drink.

But how was she going to approach the situation.

Ross decided to go for a walk down the lane.

He needed to get out of the house.

Whilst out walking he was thinking of what Charlie and his mum had, said.

As he turned the corner he noticed new neighbours' moving in.

He saw a young lad walking up to the gate he pulled himself up, and was swinging on it.

Ross noticed he walked with a limp and had a brace on his leg.

'Hello mister' he said to Ross.

Ross said hello and walked on by.

Not being in the mood for talking.

He took in the views of the fields.

There was something about them being ploughed.

The rows of soil looking freshly turned over all lined up in straight, furrows.

The worms were slithering on cracks in the soil.

Birds flew down to grab them quickly before they buried themselves, under the ground.

The willow trees were swaying elegantly in the breeze.

He could feel the whispers of the leaves.

His head was held down, like an old man in a trance,

Watching each foot step he took.

All that was on his mind was his mother's words.

Some women would have walked away?

He didn't want to lose Laura or his son.

He glanced over the hedge row on his return back to the house, to see if he could get a glimpse of the new neighbours'.

Mary arrived home early with James.

She gave James his meal, then a bath, sat down and read, him a story.

Ross sat next to them on the settee.

"Have you thought about what we said this morning Ross'.

His mum said to him.

"Yes I have maybe you're right I do need to talk to someone".

"Ross you don't know until you've tried "she replied.

"I will talk to Laura tonight "He commented.

"Her friend knows a therapist that helped her.

"Think of the future for you all as well, it can't do any harm" Replied, Mary concerned for them.

Mary stayed a while and put James to bed

Laura swung the car into the drive only to see Mary's car there.

Damn it she thought, I didn't think Mary would be back this early.

She was hoping to have some time to talk with Ross before James, was home.

Laura walked in to the house and hung her coat on the hook.

'Hello Mary' she said as she entered the kitchen.

'Have you and James had a good to time.'

'I hope he's not tired you out to much' Laura commented.

'No he's no bother keeps me young and fit' laughed Mary.

'He's fast asleep all that running around in the park has tired him out; he'll sleep well tonight "she said to Laura.

"I think I'll head of home now and have a nice relaxing bath"

"Thanks Mary for having James today"Replied Laura.

'That's ok' said Mary he's growing up so quickly'.

'Anyway I'm off see you another day, by you two she shouted, to Ross.

"Have a safe journey home and thanks again' Commented Laura.
With that Mary was on her way.

At last they were on their own, thought Laura.
They had finished their evening meal.
Laura was hesitating how to start the conversation.
"I'm going for a shower "she said to Ross.

She knew it was not going to be easy for her what she was about to,
say to Ross.

She had rehearsed it over and over in her mind during the day,
but how was she going to approach the subject.

There was really only one way straight to the point she knew it had to,
be said?

Laura came down the stairs preparing to tell Ross.

"I need to talk to you "she said to him.

"So do I you' was his reply which took Laura by surprise.
"Oh do you what about "She asked.

'Well I've been thinking I know it's not been easy for you of late'.
Said Ross.

'True right it hasn't' replied Laura harshly.
He carried on, 'I've been quite selfish only thinking off myself'.

"Maybe I do need to talk to somebody to help me move forward,
from the accident" Ross told her.

"Does your friend have the number of the therapist she talked to?
He asked.

"Why all this sudden change"
"What's brought all this on?" asked Laura.

Ross looked at Laura took a deep breath and said 'when Charlie,
came the other day he gave me a straight talking to.'

Laura couldn't say anything because she already knew about the visit,
from her dad.
Ross would have put two a two together.

Ross carried on to say, 'It made me think of what he said to me'.
'I don't want to lose you and James I love you both too much'.
'You're my world I can't live without you'.

"Mum had a go at me as well "Commented Ross.

Laura stood there in a daze this had come as a blow for her.

She was angry with herself.

Just when she had plucked up the courage to tell him she was leaving, he had to come out with this.

How could he take this moment away from her?

The frustration showed on her face.

"You don't seem pleased about it' Ross said.

"Should I be" was Laura's snappy reply.

"Well you could be more encouraging "he commented.

'Encouraging' replied Laura' 'you've got a cheek after all I have put, up with these last months'.

'You've gone around burying your head in the sand,

Instead of talking to me before now.

Ross put his arm around her.

'I'm sorry Laura I didn't mean to hurt you this way'.

"What was it you wanted to talk to me about" commented Ross."

"Nothing much it can wait. "She replied.

With that Laura walked to the kitchen trying to contain her anger.

She put the coffee in the machine.

Placing the cup on the table, she turned to Ross.

'If this is what you want 'she said to him

"I will get the telephone number from my friend.

"Let's see how this goes shall we"

Chapter 27

This was not what Laura had expected.

She put her head in her hands wondering what she was going to do, now.

Was this for real she thought?

All this time Ross ignored any advice from her and the family.

He was actually going to get some help at last.

All Laura could think about was her plans had all gone up in smoke.

She was pleased it was Friday.

She wouldn't have to go into work the next day.

Ross stayed up late at night drinking and watching a movie.

Although his mind wasn't taking it all in, he was thinking about the, next step to take.

Laura didn't hear him come up to bed.

By the time he woke up in the morning.

Laura had already put the washing out and was playing with James in, the garden.

Ross showered dressed went down stairs to make a drink as if, nothing had happened.

He read the paper and walked into the garden.

Daddy, daddy" James ran up to him shouting.

"What are you up to young man' he said to him.

I found a worm" said James.

"Wow is it a thin one or fat one" Ross commented.

James giggled and opened his hand "look a fat Worm.

"Let's put him in the garden" said Ross.

"It helps the insects from eating the vegetables".

James had a puzzled look on his face.

He screwed up his nose and put the worm on the ground,

But he's got no one to look after him daddy"
"Yes he has he's got some friend under the leaves."
His dad told him.
They walked around the garden looking for other worms.
Laura shouted through the kitchen window lunch was ready.
James sat at the table telling his mum all about the lonely worm he, found.
Laura could only listen attentively is this start she thought of better, things to come.
Josie decided it had been weeks since she saw them all.
She couldn't keep avoiding them.
She had missed taking James to the park.
Whilst pressing the button on the intercom, she was thinking what, excuse she could make.
Then she didn't need an excuse after all she was a busy woman with a, business to run.
Laura answered, and then she opened the gates.
She waited at the front door as Josie drove up the drive.
'Hello Josie' said Laura' lovely to see you come on in'.
Josie walked into the kitchen to join them, pulled out a chair and sat, down.
Coffee asked Laura, 'that would be lovely Josie replied'.
What have you been up to these past weeks' asked Ross?
'Working' Josie said 'the shops been very busy.'
'There's more weddings this time of year said Josie.
Josie sat talking to Ross, she noticed a brighter tone in his voice.
One hour had passed by.
James was running around the house with his toy airplane he had, brought back off holiday.
Josie turned to Laura, 'does my favorite boy want a trip to the, park?"Josie said.
James dropped the toy plane yes, yes please' he said to Josie all, excited.
"I'm sure he would but you don't have to' replied, Laura.

'It's no bother anyway it will give you and Ross some time together'.
James couldn't get his coat on quick enough.
 'Calm down' said Laura as she struggled to get his arm in the sleeve
of his coat.
   Meanwhile Josie collected up the cups and put them in the dishwasher
for Laura.
Ross walked into the hall behind her.
"So you've been busy have you then" Said Ross.
 Josie looked him straight in the eye.
"Yes why "she commented.
   "Oh nothing"
 "I just wondered if you had been out with your friend again'.
    You should bring him round some time it would be nice to meet
him. Ross commented.
 Josie coloured up.
'Oh its early days' she replied.
 'Any way never you mind what I've been up to Ross'.
She said trying to evade the issue,
 Work, that's what I've been up to.
 'You seem a bit brighter Ross anything you want to tell me' said
Josie.
'No replied' Ross.
 He wanted to keep things to himself at the moment.
   Josie hated herself for lying to him.
But then how could she tell him she had been seeing Jimmy.
   Laura heard all the commotion in the hall.
 "That's enough" she said to Ross.
 "Stop winding Josie up"
 'There James auntie Josie's taking you to the park now you be a good
boy', his mum told him.
With that Josie left thinking she wish she had not come, but then she
would not have the fun with James in the park.
 How long was she going to keep up the pretence?
Before they found out.
   Laura decided to sit in the sun lounge and read the paper.
Ross walked in to the hall and put his coat on.

He poked his head around the door.
"Off out then' said Laura to him.
     I'm just going for a walk." replied Ross 'Ok' she said.
   That's strange thought Laura.
   Your son's at the park with Josie, he could have taken him,
     for a walk.
   But she knew James would enjoy the swings and slides.
     Ross walked slowly down the lane.
   When he gone as far as the neighbours house.
 He saw the young lad again.
"Hello mister where are you going."He shouted.
 Ross looked up and saw he was trying to play cricket with another,
boy.
 Ross said hello and walked on by.
  He came to the wooden bench and sat for a while thinking about the,
young lad.
   When he got up to walk back home he saw him coming towards him.
"Hello again' said the boy.
"My name's Edward but you can call me Eddie,"
"What's you name mister".
"Ross" he replied.
 "We've just moved here" Eddie said to him.
"I know' replied Ross.
"I saw you the other day".
Ross wasn't really in the mood for talking.
Eddie persisted on having a conversation with him.
"My mum said the country air will do us all good".
"Did she" replied Ross.
 "My mum said it's not as noisy as living in a town and there's,
not so much traffic'.
What's the matter with your arm Eddie said to Ross?
He noticed Ross's arm was in a sling,
 Ross had covered it over with his coat.
 Ross ignored his comment.

He looked down at the boy's leg.

"What did you do to your leg"? Ross asked him.

"It was when I was born" replied Eddie.

"I'm 11 it's my birthday next week".

"Let me guess" said Ross.

"You will be 12".

"How did you know that" Replied Eddie.

"Not hard to work it out is it' commented Ross smiling.

Eddie scuffed the floor with his shoes.

"But my mum said you can do anything if you try"

"I like to play cricket with my friend.

'Maybe I'll try to play golf."

Golf thought Ross how was he going to play golf with a brace on his, leg.

"I don't know about that" said Ross.

"Oh you can because.

Ross stopped him in his tracks let me guess was it my mum said."

"How did you know I was going to say that"?

Ross replied "I just did."

"Would you like to meet my mum "? said Eddie.

"Not today" replied Ross.

"I've got to go maybe another day".

They said their goodbyes

"See you tomorrow" shouted Eddie "Maybe" said Ross.

Chapter 28

As Ross walk back to the house he thought about the,
Young lad, Eddie.
He had lived with his problem from young age.
Yet he was determined to try things in life.
If only he had his courage before now.
It made Ross feel embarrassed with himself.
The young boy didn't look at it as an obstacle.
His mother encouraged him to be like any other boy.
When Ross arrived home he told Laura about the boy he'd meet.
That had moved into the house down the road.
Laura was listening intensely she had never heard Ross talk about,
other people in that way for some time.
What was this sudden change in him?
How long will it last she thought.
All the plans she had made to leave him.
She deserved better, then so did Ross.
Realizing it wasn't his fault in the first place this had happened.
She felt trapped and could see no way forward.
Maybe she did need to give him another chance.
Then they could make some plans for the future.
But she knew her feeling had changed.
Ross also knew he had to face facts.
The last thing he wanted was Laura to leave with James.
Monday morning came Laura had dropped James off at nursery.
When she arrived at work the first thing she did was to phone her,
friend Janet.
Is this going to be a waste of time she thought to herself?
But then nothing was a waste of time if it truly meant a better life for,
Ross and the family.

She could feel the tension rising in her body whilst waiting for the, phone to be answered.

Hello Janet" she said.

I know its long time since I spoke to you.

Well it's lovely to hear your voice, said Janet 'how have you been, by the way I'm sorry to hear about Ross's accident how's he coping", replied Janet.

"We'll that what I'm calling you about said Laura.

I hope you don't mind me phoning"

'It's been a difficult time for us all I thought it would be good for Ross to talk to someone professional to help him move on from the accident'.

'You know how men are, they think they can cope and don't need any, help'.

'Anyway he's finally agreed to see someone

I hope you don't think I'm being too intrusive.'

"Do you happen to have the number of the psychologist you went to, see?'

'Give me a minute and I'll get the number for you' said Janet, she soon found the number for Laura.

Then they both caught up with all the gossip.

They were just about to end the conversation when Janet said to her, "by the way I saw Josie the other weekend."

"She was coming out of a hotel with a young man carrying a, Small suit case it looked like they had stayed the weekend'.

'Max and I had decided to go to Cornwell for a break we were just, heading off in a taxi."

'It happened so quick we didn't have time to tell the driver to wait".

"I'm sure she saw us but looked the other way."

"As if she wanted to avoid us, I noticed they were arm in arm'.

"When you see her say hello to her from me will you'.

'I will' Laura replied.

"If there's anything I can do just let me know won't you".

"Catch up soon" she said "and say hello to Ross form me and Max, will you'.

I will and thanks Janet replied Laura.

They said their goodbyes,

Laura put the phone down.

All she had to do was to phone Ross and give him the number.

The rest was up to him.

What was more on Laura's mind who had Josie been seeing.

She had not mentioned of being away for a weekend with her friend, the other day she came round.

That's strange thought Laura.

In fact she said she had been busy at work.

Laura's curiosity was getting the better of her,

She pressed the numbers on the phone waiting for Ross to answer.

'Hi Ross it's me' she said 'I've spoken to Janet this morning'

'She gave me the name and number of the psychologist".

Ross was a bit taken a back.

He didn't expect her to be that quick at getting in touch with her friend.

Just give me a minute I'll get a pen and paper and take it down' he, replied.

Laura gave Ross the telephone number.

"By the way has Josie said anything about seeing anyone?'

"Nothing serious just a friend she told me anyway, she said she had, been too busy in the shop why' commented Ross.

"It's just that Janet said she saw her coming out of a hotel with a, young man that's all in Cornwell'

'She was carrying a small suit case'.

'Janet said it looked as though they had been there for the weekend'.

"Strange she hasn't mentioned anything to us" Replied Laura.

Oh well suppose it's none of our business.

After all she's a grown woman.

Anyway I have to go got a board meeting.

See you later have a good day.

You too replied Ross.

Chapter 29

Ross walked up and down the hall looking at the number he had, written down.

A woman he thought.

It's not like talking man to man.

Then he couldn't be discriminating after all he hadn't met her.

She may be very good at her job.

Oh well here goes thought Ross.

He picked up the mobile entered in the telephone numbers.

Ross waited anxiously for someone to answer.

'Good Morning' the young voice said at the other end.

'Miss Reeve's secretary how may I help you'.

Ross explained he would like to make an appointment to see her.

'She has a space this Friday if you would like me to book you in', replied the receptionist.

'Yes that's ok' Ross replied.

She repeated the date and time to Ross Friday 7th at 9'00.

Ross thanked her.

Ross was thinking out loud he could get a lift in to town with Laura.

The office was only around the corner from Miss Reeve's.

His mind went back to Josie.

Who had she been seen with, and coming out off a hotel with a suit, case in her hand.

He decided to phone his mum the curiosity had got the better, of him.

When his mum answered she was surprised to hear Ross's voice at the, other end of the phone.

Usually she would be phoning him.

"What's the matter" she said.
"Nothing replied Ross"

"I just thought I would phone you."

'I made an appointment to see a Miss Reeve's.'
She's a psychologist; I'm going on Friday to talk to her.
"Don't know what good it will do."

"We'll you will never know if you don't go will you "commented,
Mary.

"This may be a turning point for you.'

"By the way mum' said Ross 'has Josie said anything about having a,
weekend away with anyone"
"Not to me why' replied Mary
"Oh it's just Laura's friend saw her coming out of a hotel with a young,
man."

'Maybe I shouldn't be telling you this' Commented Ross.

'Well she was here yesterday and she didn't mention anyone to me,
where was this' enquired his mum'
'In Cornwell' replied Ross.

'Mary was surprised as he was, well she will tell us if it gets serious',
said Mary.

They finished their conversation.

Mary was as curious as the rest wondering why Josie had not said,
anything to her about having a weekend away with her friend.

There was not a lot that Josie did not talk to her mum about.
Strange thought Mary she had not said anything to her',
Still it was her business.

Mary still wondered who it was Josie had been seeing.

As the week went by Friday came for Ross to see Miss Reeve's,
Laura dropped Ross off at the office.

As Ross walked to his appointment he was thinking of what he was,
going to say.

Ross entered the waiting room.

'Good morning' said a young lady at the desk.
'How may I help you'?

Ross gave the lady his name and time of the appointment.

'Take a seat Miss Reeve's will be with you shortly'
She replied.
Just then in walked a very smartly dressed woman.
Carrying a leather brief case.
She walked up to the receptionist desk.

'Gosh the traffic this morning gets worse Anna' she said to her.
'Well you know what it's like on a Friday everyone's shopping for the, weekend' commented Anna.

'Don't remind me' replied Miss Reeves as she collected a pile of, letters of the desk.

'By the way' said Anna your 9-00 O'clock appointment has arrived.

'Yes I did see the gentleman as I came in' was her reply.

She entered her office and browsed through the mail.
Ross waited anxiously for her to call him in her room.
The receptionist looked across at him tapping his hand,
on his knee.
A rush of anxiety came over him he was thinking what was he doing, here?

Had he made a mistake?

He wanted to leave but knew he would be doing the wrong thing to, walk out.
Just then the phone rang at the desk.

The receptionist walked over to Ross.

If you would like to come this way Mr Portland'.

'Miss Reeve's will see you now',

Ross got up from his chair and followed her.

Miss Reeve's introduced herself to Ross,

Take a seat she said to him.

Now how can I help you Mr. Portland?'

Ross looked at her I'm not sure you can he said.

Well let me be the judge of that came her reply.

Let's start from the beginning.

Ross poured his heart out talking about his golfing career the car, accident.

How it had turned his life upside down and had affected him physically, and emotionally.

He felt lost in his mind

I have all this family around me but I can't seem to move on.

He didn't want to lose Laura and James.

Maybe I've been stubborn not thinking I needed any help.

Not listening to what people have been telling me.

Then he broke down in tears.

Miss Reeve's ordered a coffee for them both.

"Sorry he said a man shouldn't cry I feel like a baby."

"Don't be sorry she said" to Ross.

"It took some courage for you to make the first step and come to see, me in the first place.

You needed to let it all out.

"In the mean time let's talk about a way forward".

They discussed plans to help Ross.

Although he knew he had to make the effort himself.

There was no half ways if he wanted to move on with his life and no, quick fixes.

It would take patience and time

Ross knew by his intuition he could put his trust in Miss Reeve's to, help him.

He was so relieved he had not got up and walked out the moment he, saw her come through the door.

'Shall we arrange another appointment for you?'
She asked Ross.

'Yes that would be good' Ross's reply.

'Very well if you see my secretary she will sort it'.

Ross thanked her for listening to him.

'That what I'm here for' she answered.

Ross asked the receptionist for the next available appointment.

The young lady looked on the computer screen 'Friday 21st at,
9 o'clock is that alright for you' Mr. Portland.
'Yes that would be fine' he answered.
The young lady took a card from a box and wrote down the date and,
time of the appointment and handed it to Ross.
Ross thanked her and went on his way.
 Ross thought he would catch the bus home for a change.
It was ages since he had been on one.
It stopped at the end of the lane where he lived.
So he would have a nice slow walk home by Eddie's house.
 Ross stepped off the bus, crossed the road and headed for home.
As he walked down the lane
 His thoughts went back to the meeting with Miss Reeves.
He felt embarrassed with himself for crying in front of her.
 She had listened to everything he was saying, and was understanding,
towards him, all that he was going through, whilst not judging him.
 He was relieved he had opened up to his feelings.
 Why had he not talked to his wife like that?
After all she had been there for him all the time.
  That evening Ross discussed with Laura about his day.
 She knew she had to support him with all he was trying to do.
 But it would be as hard for her after all he had pushed her away.
It wouldn't be the same as before.

Chapter 30

Josie put the phone down locked up the shop and headed off to her, mother's for an evening meal.

Ross and Laura had decided to join them with James.

They had just finished their meal when Laura mentioned to Josie, about Janet seeing her coming out of a hotel with a young man.

Josie face went bright red.

What had Janet seen Josie thought?

How was she going to handle this?

Did Janet know who the young man was?'

Josie got edgy.

"Yes I have been seeing someone' said Josie in a sharp voice.
'But that my business and nothing to do with anyone' she felt, embarrassed by her reply.

Laura was shocked about the harshness of Josie's manner.

What on earth was the matter with her that wasn't like Josie to talk to, her like that thought Laura?

Josie pushed her plate towards the middle of the table got up and, walked in to the kitchen.

Mary flung her napkin down on the table and followed her.

When she walked into the kitchen, Josie was standing over the sink, with her head bowed down.

"What was that all about young lady' said her mum.
"Nothing mum just leave it "commented Josie.

"Oh no young lady you go back in there and apologies to Laura. Whatever your problem is Laura certainly did not deserve to be spoken, to like that' she commented.

Josie turned to face her mum.

Taking in a deep breath, she thought to herself it's now or never.

She couldn't contain herself any more, no more secrets.

It had eaten her up inside lying to them all the time.

"You may as well know you're bound to find out sooner or later".

I've been seeing Jimmy" Mary's face went white.

"We didn't want to tell you after all, what with the accident and how, Ross felt about him not being in touch with him." "It just happened."

"All this time you and Jimmy how could you Josie.

"Mary said to her "You have to tell Ross" she said.

'What do I say to him' replied Josie.

'The truth do you not realize what this will do to him he has the, decency to know' her mum carried on saying.

'How could you be so deceitful this was not the way you were, brought up?

Mary went on to say more to her.

Phillip could hear the commotion going on in the kitchen and got up to, see what was happening.

He was as shocked as Mary when she explained what it was all about. Josie stood there in tears.

She decided her mum was right she had to tell Ross and Laura the, truth about her and jimmy.

Josie dried her eyes wiping away the mascara that had run down her, cheeks brushed her hair back from her face.

She walked back into the dining room.

Stood with her hands on the back of her chair were she had been sitting.

Looked at Ross and Laura

'Well as it's seems you are all so interested in my love life".

"Who I have been seeing you may as well know'.

She blurted it out.

Ross could not believe what he was hearing.

After all he had been through.

Thinking Jimmy hadn't been in touch and all this time he had been, seeing Josie.

Ross and Josie raised their voices at each other and harsh words were, said.

'Don't bother coming round to our house any more' Ross said to, Josie.

James started to cry.

With that Ross grabbed James coat.

'Let's go Laura' he said to her.

'I'll phone you tomorrow mum thanks for the meal Bye dad'.

Laura followed Ross with James.

Laura put James in the car seat; Ross couldn't get in the car quick, enough.

'Let's get home' he said to Laura as she got in the drivers seat.

He was lost for words at what had just happened.

He slammed the car door shut they headed for home.

'Looks like you did a good job of that' said Mary to Josie.

Phillip was torn between Josie and Ross.

Why could she not have said anything before?

This would not have happened just when Ross was trying move on.

As for jimmy what sort of friend had he been to Ross?

All the years he had known him.

Josie decided not to stay any longer.

'I'm off mum, dad, don't see me out'.

She got in her car and was on her way.

'Well that worked out well' said Philip I don't know what will, happen next we don't need this at our age'.

'Talk about things come to try us a trying time it is'.

'Now what are we going to do'.

'There's nothing we can do' replied Mary.

'There to grown up people they will have to sort it out by themselves'.

'What a day I think we both need a drink 'commented Phillip.

'So do I' replied Mary.

Josie went back to the flat and phoned Jimmy.

Jimmy tried to console her.

She wanted him to be there to hold her.

But she needed time on her own.

''If only we had not got on so well that night'.

'This would not have happened' Jimmy told her.

'Don't say that jimmy or are you having second thoughts' said Josie

'No replied Jimmy you know I love you and want to marry you'.

"I'm just thinking of you, am I worth all this hurt I'm causing.'
Replied Jimmy.

'Stop it Jimmy we won't let them tear us apart' said Josie.

'The last thing I want is for us to break up.'

'They will think they have won'.

'I won't let that happen.'

We have to be strong together'.

Jimmy could feel Josie's pain.

'Are you sure you don't want me to come over he said to her.

'No I'll be alright.'

'Especially now I've spoken to you 'don't worry'.

'I love you' said Josie.

'Love you too see you tomorrow' replied Jimmy.

With that Josie put the phone down and went for a shower.

Chapter 31

The months went by.

The family feud had brought Josie and Jimmy closer together.

Josie had decided to move in with Jimmy.

Mary and Phillip spent more time looking after James.

Although it hurt them that Josie missed seeing him and taking him to, the park.

Charlie could only be there for them, but could see both sides to the, situation.

What a mess he thought and caught in the middle was little James.

Josie had just finished serving a customer when Maggie, walked into the shop.

"Good morning Maggie "she said" I haven't seen you for a long time, how have you been."

"I'm good thank you, although I want to order a wreath for a friend's, funeral'.

She continued to tell Josie about her friend and how much she would, miss her.

'Oh dear sorry to hear about that' replied Josie.

'Yes it's must be sad losing a friend as much as losing a family'.

Maggie ordered her wreath and stood back and waited whilst Josie, served a customer.

Josie helped the lady choose some flowers for her daughter's birthday, from the containers outside the shop.

'Pink Roses' she said to Josie as she bent down to smell the fragrance, of the flower gently touching the delicate petals that was her, daughter's favorite flowers.

I'll take six with some gypsophila please' she added.

Josie lifted the roses carefully from the container took them into the, shop placing them on the counter then wrapped them in pretty pink, paper.

'Would you like a card that matches the paper to write a message on', said Josie to the customer?

'Oh that would be nice' the lady replied.

Josie handed her the card.

The lady paid for her items and left the shop feeling pleased with her, purchase.

Maggie waited until Josie had finished clearing the counter.

'I know you can tell me to mind my own business' said Maggie 'but, how are you Josie'.

'Laura did tell me all about what's been going on"

'After all she has held that family together for a long time dancing to, Ross tune.'

"Did she tell you she was going to leave him months back"?

Josie eyes lit up.

"No she never mentioned it to me'.

"Yes it was when we had come back off holiday."

Maggie realized what she had said.

"Better keep it to ourselves then said Maggie."

"Can't you get together and talk about this, after all life's too short', Maggie commented.

"Did Laura tell you Ross told me not to come round the house' replied Josie?

Maggie braced herself.

"You know we all say and do things we regret some time in our life, that's what being human is about."

'We will never get everything right all the time. Otherwise how would we build bridges?'

'How would we face challenges?'

'And you know what they say pride come before a fall.

'Think about it, anyway I have to go look after yourself' Josie.

With that Maggie left the shop.

All these quotes thought Josie.

Building fences what with Ross how was she going to do that.

Anyway it wasn't her that didn't want to go round to the house.

It was him who had stopped her.

His anger when he said those words.

"Don't come round any more she wasn't welcome in their house."

All the time Laura had stood there and never said a word.

How could she not say anything after all she had done to help with, James?

They just left the house that night without even saying goodbye to, dad.

What were those words he said about me and Jimmy?

You deserve each other.

Well so did them two.

Maybe she had made mistakes.

But had not Ross also or was he just Mr perfect.

Mum always went on about Ross's achievements.

Dad just played them down.

Never saying much about hers, he was always the blue eyed boy.

Then she wasn't being fair to her mum, after all they did have a close, mother and daughter relationship.

They had their disagreements but dad would say you two I don't know, and walk away.

Take himself off into the conservatory, sit in the chair and pick up the, paper to read.

All though we would say, he's just pretending to read it.

We would laugh and say he had his radar ears on.

He knew it would all blow over in no time.

What was she doing thinking like this.

She felt like going over to their house and letting out the secret she, knew.

So Laura was going to leave him was she?

When was she going to do that she thought.

Of all the cheek and he goes on about Jimmy.

Serve's him right if she did.

Maybe he would get what he deserved.

James came into her mind what would it be like for him if she did, leave Ross.

Would she ever see him again?

That would break all their hearts.

Josie decided to close the shop at lunch time and headed, back home.

She knew Jimmy would be there after all he had a few days before, flying out to his next tournament.

Entering the drive braking sharply the car came to a sudden halt.

She fumbled for her house keys in her hand bag.

She felt like a school girl telling secrets, Laura secret.

As she put the key in the lock Jimmy appeared round the corner of, the house.

"I thought I heard a car" he said "skidding in the drive "what's the, matter with you".

Josie couldn't wait to tell him all that Maggie had told her.

How Laura was going to leave Ross.

They both sat at the kitchen table, Josie stared in to the bottom of the, coffee cup.

She had told Jimmy about Maggie coming in to the shop that morning.

"What are you thinking Josie "said Jimmy?

"I don't know anymore said Josie.

When I go to mum and dad's they keep saying you should sort it out, between you and Ross."

"But why should I be the first to give in."

"After all he threw the paddy like a spoilt child not giving me time to, explain anything about us two".

"I'm sorry Josie it's my entire fault the accident and you two falling, out.

"Don't get me wrong I love you and want to spend the rest of my life, with you."

"I know Ross always thought I was jack the lad.

"But I never thought I would feel this way about you" said Jimmy.
"Who would have thought this was going to happen between us two I,
love you so much Jimmy".

"Ross can't tear us apart I won't let him" Replied Josie.

Maybe we should both go together and sort it out said Jimmy.

"Let's not rush into anything I have to pick the right moment to see,
Ross' said Josie.

Josie knew it would not be easy facing Ross not after the row at his,
mothers.

Jimmy and Josie settled down watching the TV.

Her mind was on James.

Why had Laura not tried to contact her?

She could have phoned.

It involved all of us and in the middle little James and she missed him,
so much.

I bet she decided about leaving Ross when she went to Spain on,
holiday with Maggie thought Josie.

Her mind was doing cart wells.

Had Maggie got something to do with it all did she encourage her to,
leave?

It's a good thing mum didn't know about all this going on.

Ross took his walks daily by Eddie's house.

Looking for him and watching him try to play cricket with his friends.

Trying to run like the other boys and score points.

Ross sat on the bench under a large willow tree.

Watching the branches swaying calmly in the breeze it was so relaxing.

He could feel the rustling of the leaves.

So relaxing he closed his eyes drifting in to sleep.

Then he felt a presence near him scuffing the grass.

It made him jump 'Sorry' said Eddie' was you dozing off.'

Ross looked up' what are you doing here' he said.

'I've lost my cricket ball, did you hear it go passed your feet I'm sure it, landed there'.

"No' replied Ross."

"Ok said Eddie 'you're sure you didn't.'

"No Eddie but I'll help you look for it"

With that Ross got off the seat to help Eddie look for his ball.

"Here it is in the tuft of grass' said Ross.

'Thank you' said Eddie grabbing the ball then rushing off to his friends.

"Found it" he shouted to them all excited.

Ross took a slow walk back to the house on his way he stopped to, watch Eddie.

They were all laughing about enjoying themselves fooling around like, boys should do.

Nothing stopped Eddie.

How can a young lad have so much enthusiasm and here's me a grown, man feeling sorry for myself?

Why couldn't he be more like Eddie?

But then Ross had a career and that had been taken from him one he, loved.

It was his lively hood.

He had been financially dependent on it.

He had to adjust with his injuries.

With only having the use of one arm this not only affected him, physically, but emotionally.

He had to learn to everything with the use of one arm.

He had missed out of some things other parents would do for their, children.

He had relied on Laura and the rest of the family to drive him where, he wanted to go most of the time.

Eddie had grown up with his disability not that it stopped him trying, to do anything.

It was as if his brain was programmed to go, go, go, all the time.

Where did he get his energy from?

His mind wondered to James what he would be like when he was,
Eddie's age and what games he would play.

Things were swirling round his head.

What Laura had said about getting in touch with Josie and Jimmy?

He too had missed Josie more than he let on.

It had taken its toll on all the family.

They had to pick their times to visit hoping he wasn't going to bump,
in to her.

It was all so stupid.

Why did he have to lose his temper like that and walk out the house in,
a foul mood?

What on earth did his mum and dad think about it all?

He didn't care at the time.

This had knocked him back and he was angry with himself telling,
Josie not to come round.

James had missed her and kept asking when Auntie Josie was coming,
to see him.

Why doesn't she come did she not love him anymore.

The tears would swell up in his eyes when he spoke those words.

Ross would reply she's very busy with her flowers.

Knowing to well he was lying to his son, how could he do this to him.

That was no way to bring up a child he thought.

But then he was too young to understand about adult life.

It was Friday afternoon Laura was leaving work early to go to the,
grocery store.

She switched off the computer tidied her desk.

Slung her coat across her shoulder and picked up her bag.

She poked her head round the corner of Rosie's office.

"See you Monday have a good weekend."

"You too" replied Rosie.

With that she headed for the car park.

The traffic was busy on a Friday afternoon.

Trying to get through town people were getting agitated.

Slow older drivers were holding up the young ones causing them to,
hoot their car horns at them.

For goodness sake some drivers have no patience thought Laura has a, young lad cut in front of her.

He gave her a smirky look then stuck two fingers up at her.

'You too she shouted to him I might see you in court one of these days, then who's the clever one.'

Chapter 32

Laura gave a sigh of relief as she entered the grocery store car park.

She looked for a parking space she knew it would be busy this time of, day.

She lifted up the car boot and took out the shopping bags.

She was just going to put the coin in the trolley when she spotted, Josie coming through the door.

They both stopped in their tracks and starred at each other.

Now who's going to say the first word thought Josie?

She bit her lip waiting in anticipation.

Well' she's not she thought.

The seconds went by sod it thought Josie.

With that she walked up to Laura.

Hello Laura how are you Josie said to her.

Laura felt uneasy especially after the incident with the young driver in, town.

'I'm ok "replied Laura.

"Really' commented Josie in a sarcastic tone.

Now Josie knew what Maggie had told her she wanted to find out for, herself.

"Why shouldn't I be" replied Laura.

Josie couldn't resist it "It's just I bumped in to Maggie the other day, and she told me something very interesting" commented Josie.

Laura grew anxious but kept her calm.

She could feel the tension rising in her breast.

'What might that be then Josie' she replied.

"Well I was wondering if you and Ross were getting on alright."

"Were fine and what's it to you' commented Laura.

"Nothing should it be."Josie replied.

Now Josie knew she was being bitchy but couldn't help herself.

It was if she was enjoying every minute of the conversation.
She had got something on Laura that Ross didn't know.

"When were you going to tell Ross you were leaving him?" said,
Josie.

Too late she had blurted it out.

She knew she should have kept her mouth shut.

Laura was stunned she knew where the information had come from.

Maggie, she was the only one who knew about it.

How could she do that to her she thought, to Josie of all people.

That was the last person she didn't want her to tell.

She trusted her not to say anything to anyone.

Now that trust had been broken.

"What did Maggie tell you" replied Laura.

"Enough said Josie."

"Anyway Laura you never said anything on the night Ross walked out,
at mums."

"Do you know how that hurt her?"

"It's not my fault Jimmy hasn't been in touch with Ross"

'Who I go out with is nothing to do with him'.

'Ross certainly made it crystal clear I was not welcomed in your,
house anymore'.

'You just stood there and never said a bloody word like a puppet on a,
string being pulled along at his demand'.

Laura was feeling unnerved by it all.

She was worried that Ross would find out that she was going to leave,
him.

This was the last thing she needed.

Wondering was there anything going to go right for her in her life.

Laura felt embarrassed standing outside a grocery store discussing all,
their dirty laundry in public what if someone from work had seen them.
With Josie in such a temper it wouldn't surprise her if she went straight,
home and phoned Ross.

"Do you know Josie said Laura how hard it's been for me since the, accident?"

"I've prayed every night things would get better for us."

"I don't know how I've had the strength to carry on sometime."

"But I had to for James sake."

"I had to talk to someone although I thought Maggie was a friend I, could confide in."

"But obviously not."

Josie knew she had made a mistake blurting it out.

Damn it she said to herself me and my big mouth.

Instead of trying to sort things out she had made worse of it.

I'd better go said Laura.

With that she pushed the trolley in to the store.

Her mind wasn't on the shopping list.

She just threw things in the trolley not bothered what she picked up.

All she was thinking was how much had Maggie told Josie.

She couldn't wait to pay for her groceries and get out the store.

She rammed the groceries into the shopping bags.

After paying for them she made her way back to the car, the groceries, were loaded into the boot.

She pulled out the car park and headed towards home.

But she wasn't going to go home she had made up her mind, she swung the car round and headed for Maggie's place.

Pulling in to the drive she saw her standing by the garage.

Maggie walked up to the car.

" Hello Laura what brings you here this time of day is anything the, matter."

'Anything the matter you should ask' said Laura.

"What do you mean?" said Maggie.

"Well you fill in the gaps, 'I've just seen Josie at the grocery store we, had a very interesting conversation.

Maggie knew straight away what was coming next.

"Oh dear "she replied.

"Is that all you can say Maggie.

'Oh dear".

'I trusted you and confided in you as a friend'.

'You let me down Maggie how could you have done that to me.'

Laura burst in to tears 'why did you do it'.

'Now she will tell Ross and I don't want him to know I was going to, leave him'.

"He's tried so hard lately".

"This will be the last straw".

"I'm sorry Laura' said Maggie 'I didn't mean to let it out."

"Please forgive me I don't want to lose our friendship"

"What can I do to make it right?"

'You can't the damage has been done'.

'Nothing will make anything right' replied Laura.

'You'll never know how sorry I am for telling Josie', replied Maggie.

Laura stood there in silence for a moment.

"I have to go Maggie, 'James will want his evening meal".

'You know Laura maybe it's time you all got together and sorted it, out.'

'You will never be able to forgive each other until it's done once and, for all'

'If I had not gone in that shop that day none of this would have, happened between us.'

'But I did I'm sorry to break the trust we had'.

With that Maggie walked into the house and closed the door behind, her.

She heard Laura's car pull off out of the drive.

She wondered if she would ever see her again.

She clasped her head in her hands and sobbed her heart out.

Laura stopped the car up the road to refresh her makeup.
The last thing she wanted was for Ross to see she had been crying.
What a day she thought when she pulled up in to the driveway.
Ross had seen her car enter the drive and was waiting at the door.
Laura opened the car boot picking up the bag of groceries.
'Hello love he said your late is everything alright'.
'Yes it was busy with the traffic in town and the grocery store' she, replied.
She was not going to tell Ross about Josie and about seeing Maggie.
She had had enough for one day.
All she wanted to do was sort out a meal for them all,
Put James to bed and then have an early night.
She knew she had to speak to Josie before Ross found out anything.
But when she thought and how, it was another mess to sort out.
Laura lay awake, most of the night trying to work out a plan to see, Josie and Jimmy together.
She could deal with the problems that happened in court.
But when it came to her problem's that was another matter.
This had split the family it was such a mess she did not need any of, this.
Other family's have problems thought Laura.
Maybe I should have left when I had the chance.
Things would have been different in so many ways.

Chapter 33

Ross had come out of Miss Reeve's office.

He had just finished having another consultation with her.

As he turned the corner he stood looking at Josie across the road.

She was arranging some flowers in the shop window.

Was he going to cross the road and go in or walk on by?

He thought about how much they had all missed each other and what he had said in his anger.

How he wished he could turn the clock back on many occasions.

His mind went back to how he and Josie used to play in the garden, when they were young.

How they would tease each other.

There were good family times together.

How life had changed.

He knew he had to let go of the past if he wanted to move forward.

He had tried hard with the help of his counselling although it had been, a struggle at times.

It was hard to accept what had happened in the past and come to, terms with how things were now.

He wondered how Laura had put up with his moods.

Realizing it had not been easy for her.

He had to look beyond hope.

He fumbled with his hand in his coat pocket rattling the loose coins, together.

'Here we go' he said to himself.

He waited for the traffic to clear then crossed the road and walked into, the shop.

Josie looked up from the counter when she heard the door open.

She was not in any mood for another row she thought as she, saw Ross walk in.

She kept quiet waiting for Ross to say the first word.

The atmosphere was tense.

Who was going to make the first move?

What do they say he thought pride comes before a fall?

He had to swallow his pride.

He walked up to her put his arm around her.

   "I'm sorry' he said "and cried on her shoulder.

This started Josie off crying.

   "So am I "cried Josie 'What a mess'.

 I've missed you Josie' said Ross.

So have I' In fact I've missed all of you' said Josie.

'How's James? She asked him.

   'Missing you he keeps asking when you are coming to see him',
answered Ross.

 He asks when is Auntie Josie coming to take me to the park.

'It's been hard not seeing him' she told Ross.

   "I know, let's get together and talk" Ross said,

'Ok, I'll call you this weekend when I have finished work.'

 'Oh now look at me my mascara's run, I must look a mess' she said,
trying to wipe her eyes

'What will the customers think if they see me like this?'

 'Stop fussing you look lovely sis' Ross told her as he wiped a tear,
from her eye.

 Flattery will get you every where big brother 'she Laughed.

'I'll be in touch' he said and gave her a kiss on the cheek.

 He smiled at her as he left the shop.

 Feeling pleased with himself that he had plucked up the courage to see,
Josie.

   When Laura arrived home that evening he told her all about it.

 All that was going through Laura's mind was what had they discussed?

Had Josie told Ross what Maggie had told her?

Had she mentioned their argument in the store car park?

She suspected not, as he seemed in too good a mood.

 The last thing she wanted was for him to find out about it all.

 The panic set in.

She was aware that Ross wanted Josie to call round.

So she decided she would phone Josie first, and make an excuse to, meet up.

Then she could slip it in to the conversation without him knowing.

But then would Josie tell him anyway?

The next morning Laura phoned her work colleague.

She informed her that she would be in later that morning.

Not letting on it was anything to do with the family.

She had decided to go to the shop and speak to Josie.

Ross had taken the first move to patch things up between them.

Now how was she going to approach the subject after all the incident, at the grocery store was nothing to shout about?

Well if anything it was Josie doing the shouting not her.

Laura parked the car and headed for the shop.

Looking through the window she could see Josie had some, customers inside.

She would wait until they had gone before going in,

She picked up a bunch of flowers from the containers outside, the shop and walked up to the counter.

"Hello "she said casually.

"I'll take these."

Josie looked Laura in the eye as she wrapped the flowers.

As Laura handed her the money she caught Josie's hand.

"Josie Ross told me he had been to see you".

"Yes "she replied casually.

"That was nice of him."

I'm pleased for you both' she said to Josie.

'Maybe you would like to come to lunch on Sunday?

'That's if you want to' she said.

Josie couldn't believe what she was hearing.

Why all of this sudden change of heart from Laura.

After the disagreement they had.

But she did not want any more arguments; there had been enough, upsets in the past.

"That would be nice I'll phone you on Friday to confirm' said Josie.
 "Well phone me at the office if you can make it, I can arrange,
    to do the shopping on my way home from work".
   Laura knew she had to be tactful full about getting round to the
subject, before Josie spoke to Ross.
"Ok will do" replied Josie.
 Laura left and headed for work knowing she had to have a plan.

Chapter 34

Friday came and as arranged Josie phoned Laura at lunch time to say,
she would be coming for lunch on Sunday.

"There is one thing I need to talk to you about first"
Josie said.

Laura hesitated "what's that? She asked.

Wondering what the next words were going to be.

"I can't talk now let's have a coffee in town Saturday lunch time I'll,
tell you then' Said Josie.

"Ok" agreed Laura.

Then they both hung up.

Laura didn't tell Ross about the Saturday lunch time arrangement,
with Josie.

She only told him about her coming for lunch on Sunday.

She knew she had one last chance to broach the subject she had to take,
it.

All night she tossed and turned anxious about the conversation.

The next day nervously she walked into the coffee shop.

Josie was sitting near the window looking out at the tubs full of,
flowers.

The flowers were looking quite droopy.

Bet they haven't been watered for a while she thought.

Maybe they need some feed.

Still, that was not what she was there for.

Just then Laura turned up.

Laura pulled out a chair and sat down opposite her.

"Hello Josie have you been waiting long' she asked
"No, I was just admiring the flowers.

'Or shall I say the disappointing look of them said Josie.

'Oh yes' replied Laura as she glanced at them.

The young waiter came over to the table.

'Can I take your order ladies 'he asked them?

"Coffee for me" said Josie.

"The same for me" replied Laura.

"Anything else' he asked.

"No thank you" they both replied.

Off he went to sort out the coffees,

"This is my lunch hour' said Josie 'so I don't have too much time'.

Laura clasped her hand together.

Here goes she thought.

Josie spoke first.

"Look Laura, 'I know it was wrong keeping it from you that I was, seeing Jimmy'

I'm not making any excuses for him but he's been hurting too'.

'He knows that he was responsible for the accident and he feels bad for, what happened to Ross'

He couldn't' face it all, and felt he had to get away for a while'.

"We've tried to walk away from each other unfortunately you can't, help who you fall in love with.

"No matter how much people think you're doing the wrong thing. I can't and won't give him up."

"I love him and he loves me in fact were going to get married.

'I know it sounds crazy'

"I'm not sure how to tell Ross' Josie explained to Laura.

Laura was gob smacked at what she had just heard?

Josie was getting married to Jimmy, who would have thought, that would happen.

Just then the young man returned and placed the coffees on the table. They both thanked him, and off he went.

Laura stirred her coffee turning the spoon round and round in the cup. She was thinking about the times she had sat in the same seat, with Maggie opposite her.

'You'll wear a hole in the cup" said Josie.

Laura looked up.

'Sorry, I was thinking.'

'I know you were miles away' smiled Josie.

"When you said you wanted to meet up I was wondering what you, were going to say.

This has come as a shock' replied Laura.

"But I'm sure there's a way we can sort this in time."

Now Laura had the upper hand.

Josie needed her help.

"Let me talk to Ross' she suggested.

It's about time he and Jimmy got together" Laura said.

"It won't be easy for them, but they're two grown men and it's gone, on long enough "said Laura.

"There's just one thing Josie" asked Laura.

"What's that?   Josie asked.

Well you know the other day at the grocery store' said Laura.

"Yes" replied Josie

"I don't want Ross to ever find out that I was thinking of leaving him."

"At that time I was at my wits end, struggling with a job and trying to, hold a family together".

"Things were in a bad way for Ross and me, so much, that I was, finding it hard to cope' continued Laura.

'But since then he has been going to therapy and he's starting to get, more positive in himself."

"I don't want him to take a step back.

He needs to keep moving forward and stay positive, she told her.

"I understand" said Josie.

"I won't say anything let's put that behind us."

Laura breathed a sigh of relief.

Thank goodness for that she thought.

But how was she going to approach Ross about meeting up with, Jimmy?

But needs must and she would do it for all their sakes.

'Before you come on Sunday Josie, you have to talk to Jimmy' Laura, told her.

"Would he be willing to come to lunch on Sunday?

"I don't know it might not go down well with Ross" said Josie.

"We have only just started talking to each other."

You leave it to me said Laura.

I'll phone you later.

'Ok if you say so' replied Josie 'but be it on your head'.

Josie reached for Laura's hand.

'Thank you for being so understanding' she said to her.

'You too' replied Laura.'

They drank their coffees and both left together,

Josie returned to open the shop.

Laura knew she had done the right thing meeting up with Josie.

Now she could concentrate on broaching the subject to Ross.

She had made a truce with Josie and was determined to carry out her, plan.

Chapter 35

James was put to bed a little early that evening.

Laura knew it was now or never.

If they were coming to lunch on Sunday she had to do it now.

"Ross, sit down please' she said.

"I need to have a serious conversation with you."

"Before you say anything hear me out".

Laura told him about Josie and Jimmy, apart from one particular, piece of information

"I think it's time you all got together.

'This needs to be sorted out once and for all".

The colour drained from his face.

"Are you serious' he asked her'

"I am more than serious" replied Laura sternly.

'In fact I'm telling you that I'm fed up with this bickering and step, toeing around the family.'

'We need to have some stability in our life.

Something for the future'

'Not just for you, but for James'.

'He needs to see Josie, she's family and family is important'.

'It's not fair to bring him in to all of this and he's missing out on all the, fun he has with her.

"It won't be easy" Ross said.

"Who said everything would be easy in life, we know that' replied, Laura.

'I think you should call Jimmy tonight' she told him.

Ross knew Laura was right in what she had said.

He was very anxious as he waited for Jimmy to answer his phone.

What was he going to say?

He had not been prepared for this.

It seemed to take a long time before Jimmy answered.

'Hello Jimmy' said Ross.

There was a silent pause the other end of the line.

"I didn't expect you to phone me' said Jimmy surprised.

"No' replied Ross.

'I thought it was time we both got in touch'.

'It's been a long time since we had a conversation' said Ross',

'I know' replied Jimmy.

'You haven't been in touch with me since the accident.
I would have thought you could have at least phoned me to see,
how I was getting on' said Ross'

"Sorry Ross I know I should have called before now'.

'Yes well I needed to talk to you' said Ross.

They discussed the conversation about Laura seeing Josie.

"Come over for lunch with Josie on Sunday' he told Jimmy.

"Are you sure that's what you want' asked Jimmy.

"Yes 'replied Ross.

'Ok then I will' said Jimmy.

They arranged a time to get together.

Jimmy placed his phone on the table.

"Who was that "Josie Asked?' although she already knew.

It was Ross he wants us to go round theirs for lunch this Sunday' he,
told Josie

'So what did you say to him' asked Josie.

I told him that we would go'

"That's a start "Josie replied.

"We'll be alright I'm here by your side" she told him.

"I know you are but, Josie stopped him in his tracks.

"There's no buts were going"

Laura was pleased Ross had phoned Jimmy, it was a break through.
She was wondering what Ross would say to him regarding the,
accident,

Bringing it all up again old wounds take time to heal.

Sunday came and Jimmy drove into the drive.

They were both anxious and nervous about Jimmy approaching Ross.

What was he going to say, he hadn't spoken to Ross since the, accident?

Not until the short telephone conversation yesterday.

Jimmy picked up the bottle of wine from the back seat of the car.

Josie had brought some flowers for Laura.

She slipped her arm in his and they walked up to the front door, together.

Josie could hear James running to the door as she approached the step.

When Laura opened the door, James pushed past his mum.

'Hey young man' she said laughing, where's your manners.

'Auntie Josie' he said jumping up with excitement.

'Hello young man' said Josie, 'what are you up to?

With that she bent down to give him a peck on the cheek.

How she had missed him and their trips to the park,

She missed James having fun on the slides and roundabouts and his, giggling as she pushed him higher on the swing.

'Let Josie and Jimmy come through the door then' said Laura to, James.

He's too excited that's his trouble'.

Laura took their coats.

Josie handed the flowers to Laura.

'They are lovely you didn't have to bring anything.'

'I know, but I wanted to' said Josie.

'Well thanks anyway' replied Laura, I'll just put them in a vase'.

I'm just making coffee would you like one, or something else to, drink?

"Coffee's fine' they both replied.

'Ross is in the conservatory Jimmy' said Laura.

Go in and take a seat you can give him the bottle of wine'.

"Do you need any help" asked Josie.

"You can come in the kitchen if you want let's leave the men to talk.'

'James is busy helping with the cooking'.

"Well making a mess with the flour anyway.

Josie rubbed her hands threw James's hair.

'Well young man what are you busy doing? Asked Josie.

I'm making a pie "answered James as he rolled the pastry over and, over again.

The flour was all over the table but James insisted in rolling the pastry, out by himself.

The more mess he made the more excited he was.

'Now what sort of pie is it' Josie asked.

'Jam, strawberry jam' said James.

'Don't you mean jam tarts'?

'No, I told you Jam pie' said James.

'Ok if you say so James' replied Josie laughing.

'Would you like me to help you' Josie asked.

'Let Josie help you with the pastry' his mum told him,

'Ok' James replied.

Josie washed her hands and put on an apron.

"Now if I lift the pastry in the dish' said Josie 'you can put the jam in, what do you say to that?"

Josie lifted the pastry into the dish smoothed it out, and made a pattern, on the edge of the pastry with a fork.

James couldn't get the jam in quick enough, it dropped off the spoon, all over the table, Josie had to scoop it up and put it in the pie.

All Laura could do was laugh at them both.

By the time it was ready to put in the oven Josie was covered in flour, as well as James.

'Do you want some when it's cooked'? James said to Josie.

'Of course I do James especially if you've made it'

Josie winked at Laura.

'I hope you know what you're letting yourself in for Josie?' Laura said to her.

'It will be alright', said Josie laughing.

'Any way we can all have some can't we James' Josie asked.
Laura stood there open mouth.
   'You'd better give Auntie Josie the biggest piece' Laura told him.
'Yes she can have the biggest piece' he replied.
Josie winked at him then she gave him a hug.
Wondering what she had let herself in for.
   Let's get cleaned up and ready for lunch she told James.

   Jimmy walked into the conservatory.
He was wondering what reception he would get from Ross.
   Ross got up from his chair 'nice to see you at last he said to Jimmy'.
Jimmy felt awkward for a moment 'yes I know he answered' then,
handed Ross the bottle of wine.
   'Thanks Jimmy' Ross said as he took the bottle from him 'we can,
have this later with our meal'.
'It's been a while now since we saw each other.
'I thought this day would never come again 'said Ross.
Jimmy felt the anxiety kick in.
A grilling, that's what he thought he was going to get from Ross.
"I'm sorry I haven't been in touch Ross' said Jimmy.
"I know I have no excuses".
"I just couldn't face you after the accident"
"Also, with your surgery it got too much for me."
"I had to get away' said Jimmy.
   "Well, you could at least have phoned' said Ross'
"Do you think it's been easy for me? He asked Jimmy.
 "No' was Jimmy's reply."
   Jimmy wished he had not have come.
 They started to raise their voices things weren't going so well.
   Laura came into the conservatory with the coffee on a tray,
hearing the commotion she was not pleased with Ross.
   They had come to make a truce not start another family row.
   'What's going on?' she asked.
"I can hear you in the kitchen.

It's no good getting angry with each other."
"This doesn't solve anything; for goodness sake you're,
  grown men.
'We are not having this all afternoon'
They're here for lunch lets all behave like civilised adults."
'Also, it's not good for James to hear all this going on.
 Ross knew she was right.
  "Sorry Jimmy' he said.
'Laura's right, 'let's have our coffee.
Laura walked back in to the kitchen.
 'Don't worry' she said to Josie smiling 'I soon sorted those two out'.
Now let's see if James pie cooked shall we.
Things settled down, the shouting had stopped and they were talking,
civilised to each other.
 'I must admit, I've missed our drinking time together'
Said Jimmy
"I can still lift a pint "replied Ross.
"I can pick you up at the weekend and we can go for a pint at the local,
pub' said Jimmy.
 'That's if you want to come with me?' asked Jimmy.
'Or Laura can drop you off'.
 "I'll sort it out, but I will take you up on the drink".
 Ross told him.
 Jimmy enquired about the extent of his surgery.
 Not letting on to Ross what Josie had told him?
 'Ross went on to say,' I get agitated because I can't do what I could,
with my arm'.
"It will never be the same."
"I damaged the nerves in the accident so have limited use,"
"I get scared what the future will hold for us all' continued Ross.
 'I'm pleased you both came' said Ross to Jimmy.
"I don't want to fall out with you, it's not easy having to adjust" said,
Ross.

"I know it can't be easy." commented Jimmy.

"Sorry Ross this is my fault entirely'.

'I feel guilty every day, knowing what I've done to you and your, family."

"It hasn't been easy for me carrying that burden around in my head."

"Well you were driving, was Ross's reply, realizing what he had said, he quickly changed the subject."

The two talked some more and felt more at ease with each other.

Chapter 36

'Lunch is ready' shouted Laura from the kitchen.
They made their way to the dining room.

"Auntie Josie you sit next to me" James said.
'Alright I will' said Josie.

But you've got to eat all your vegetables' Josie told James'
Jimmy sat the other side of Josie.

'Help yourself' Laura said to them', but make sure you leave room for,
the pudding especially as James's made it.

'Yes and Auntie Josie's having the biggest piece' James told them.
'I can't wait' answered Josie smiling at James.

Ross poured the wine and they all enjoyed the chit chat around the,
table, like old times.

'What's the secret Laura to your roast potatoes there so fluffy in the,
middle and lovely and crisp on the outside, asked Josie?
'Practice 'she replied.

'Better give Josie some tips Laura' said Jimmy.

'Don't be cheeky', Josie told him, or you'll be eating out every night'.

Josie braced herself she knew it was the right time to bring up the,
subject about her and Jimmy.

'I've got something to tell you both' she said looking at Ross.

Laura knew what was coming.

'Jimmy and I are getting married' shared Josie.

Ross nearly choked on his wine, spluttering it across the table.
James giggled as he looked at his daddy.

Mr Messy' said Laura.

Laura knew she had to say something quick.

"Let's raise our glasses to Josie and Jimmy".

"Congratulations to you both."

Ross followed along with it "Congratulations" he said.
They all chinked their glasses together.

James also chinked his glass full of orange juice with them they all, laughed and smiled at him.

"When did all this happen then? Ross asked Jimmy.

"It just did over time" Jimmy replied.

'I know it's not what you expected Ross.'

'But Josie and I love each other' he told Ross.

'Well it's not what Ross wants it's what you two want; replied Laura.

As long as you two are both happy that's all that matters.

Isn't it Ross?'

Ross agreed with her for once.

'After all it's the future that count's, for all of us'.

'Not the past" said Laura.

Josie was surprised at how Laura had handled it all.

Thanking her for her support for them both.

How grateful she was for this moment.

The rest of the day went peacefully along.

Josie read a bed time story to James.

Then she tucked him up in bed like old times.

When it was time to leave Ross turned to Josie.

'I'm so pleased you both came' he told her.

He knew Josie looked happy with Jimmy.

Maybe they were a perfect match.

'Just one thing Jimmy' said Ross

Everyone was waiting to hear what Ross was going to say.

"The best man" he continued.

'Well I think I'd make a good speech' winking at Josie.

'You're on' said Jimmy.

'Of Course, we will have to have a drink on it 'said Ross,

Where are you living now' asked Ross.

I've just' he stopped for a second looked at Josie continuing the, conversation, 'or should I say we have moved into a three bedroom, house in town'.

It's still only a walking distance from the pub Jimmy replied.

Josie joined in to say 'You should all come over sometime for a meal.
 'We can go for a drink' suggested Jimmy winking at Ross.
'Yes, that would be nice for us' answered Ross.
 Jimmy looked at Josie, 'well time we were off 'he said.
'Yes, was Josie's reply 'I've got a busy day tomorrow?'
 Jimmy stood up and looked out the window.
'You have a lovely little boy Ross, and a very understanding wife,
look after them both' said Jimmy.
 'I will' said Ross 'you take care and don't forget the pint you owe me'.
'I won't, replied Jimmy and they shook hands.
 Laura thanks for the lovely meal' said Josie.
Josie put her arms around Laura.
"We've had a lovely time'.
"So have I' Laura replied.
"We should catch up in the week' suggested Josie'.
"Yes we should replied Laura'
 They all said good bye and were pleased the day ended happier than it,
had started.
 Ross and Laura sat in the lounge having a night cap.
'Well it all seemed to go well in the end with you and Jimmy' said,
Laura.
 Let's hope we can put it all behind us now and move on'
 'Yes It was good to talk to him face to face and air our grievances',
agreed Ross.
 'Did you see Josie face when she got the biggest piece of pie' Laura,
said laughing?
 She daren't leave any of it for the fear of upsetting James'.
 'Well what did you expected when James kept on saying to her,
It's lovely auntie Josie;
 'You have to eat it all up like a good girl' said Ross sniggering.
 'How cute of him' replied Laura?
'I don't think Josie thought that about him at that time' answered Ross.
 Laura decided to go and check on James.
 'Sweet dreams' she said 'as she bent down and kissed him on his,
forehead'.

He stirred as she was going out the door.

'When's Auntie Josie coming again' asked James.

 'Soon, don't worry she will take you to the park next time'.

'Night, night my boy' Laura said to James.

 He yawned and closed his eye's

 Laura had taken a few days off work she was ready for a break.

 She still felt the sadness.

 The sadness of losing the friendship of Maggie.

If only she had not gone to her house that day.

 But she was raging mad when she left the super market,

that Maggie had let it slip to Josie, about her planning to leave Ross.

 She should have waited until things had calmed down.

 Maggie had been there for her, a shoulder to cry on.

 Laura had said such harsh words in her temper to her.

She was upset at the time, Maggie had betrayed her trust.

 Maggie tried her best to say how sorry she was.

Laura knew that by the look on her face.

 Maggie's eyes were full of tear that day she knew she would not win,

with Laura whatever she said to her.

So she just went into the house.

 Why couldn't she have discussed it more with her?

Rather than leaving the way she had done.

 The last thing she heard was that Maggie had sold her house to live in, Spain.

She couldn't talk to Ross

After all what would he make of it all?

So she had to suffer in silence.

The mistake was made there was nothing she could do.

 Now that Josie was on speaking terms with Ross.

 There was no way she was going to upset things.

Chapter 37

Ross woke early in the morning thinking about what Jimmy had said, about meeting up for a pint.

He knew that he had missed the conversations had with him.

After breakfast he played with James and walked round the garden. Laura prepared lunch. Ross decided to go for his walk along the lane. He took James with him.

'Hello' Ross' shout's out the young lad. Is that your little boy?' asked, Eddie.

'Do you want to see me play cricket?

'My dad's got some old golf club from his friend so I can learn to, play" 'continued Eddie 'has he' said Ross.

James watched the boy's play cricket he was jumping up and down, trying to copy them catching the ball.

Ross stood there thinking how can this young boy have so much, enthusiasm to try things with his disability?

But to Eddie he didn't have any disability.

He had grown up with learning to adapt to life with all the, encouragement from his parents.

They had taught him never to be any different from all the other boys.

Here I am at my age feeling sorry for myself, Ross thought to himself.

'Well' do you want to watch or not?' said the lad.

'Yes' said Ross.

He stood and watched as Eddie hit the ball, trying to run before his, friend hit the wicket. 'Out' shouted his friend 'Out' shouted James, trying to copy the boys.

Just then his mother came to see what the noise was all about.

She noticed Ross with James watching the boys.

'Hello' I'm Eddie's mum Sarah' she said.

He told me he sometimes talks to you while you're out walking'.

Ross introduced himself to Sarah.

Looking at James and' who might this young man be, she asked.

James moved behind his dad shying away.

'His names James, 'say hello to the lady', Ross told him.

'Oh don't upset him she replied'.

'He's shy' commented Ross.

Ross put his arm around James to comfort him.

'Would you like to come in for a drink and meet Eddie's father?' asked, Sarah.

'I don't know we don't want to interrupt your day' Ross replied.

'Of Course you won't, come along Gregg would be pleased to meet, you'.

'Well that's very nice of you' replied Ross.

Ross and James followed Sarah to her house.

Sarah walked into the lounge Sarah's husband was reading the daily, paper.

'Gregg, this is Ross and James his son the neighbours from up the, road', she said,

He rose from the chair and held his hand out to greet Ross.

'Pleased to meet you' he said to Ross.

'Sarah would you make some drinks dear?' asked Gregg'

'Would you like tea or coffee Ross' asked Sarah?

'Coffee please' replied Ross.

'How do you like it milk and sugar' she asked Ross. 'Just milk no, sugar thank you' was his reply.

'And what would this young man like' she said looking at James.

'Would you like some juice'?

James moved closer to Ross. He whispered in his ear, 'orange please, daddy'.

'Orange, please Sarah for James that would be nice thankyou'.

With that Sarah went off to sort out the drinks'

Gregg and Ross talked for a while.

They had quite a conversation about Eddie.

'He's just a typical boy getting into mischief like his friends' said, Gregg we try and encourage him not to be any different'. 'Eddie's mother was a school teacher she decided a few years, ago she would; give up teaching at the school to teach Eddie from home'.
'Eddie gets tired easily during the day this was a better option.
She also teaches some other children privately, so he can still mix and, play with them were both proud of how far he's come on in life?' said Gregg.
'I know' Ross told him 'he's always saying my mum said' they all, had a good laugh about it.
Sarah brought in the coffee and juice James kept turning around, to look at the boys laughing outside.
Just then Eddie came running in.
'Can we all have a drink please mum?' Ok.
'Yes, give me a minute' his mother replied. 'Ok' said Eddie.
Eddie stood and looked at James.
James was sitting on the floor looking at some books of Eddie's.
'Do you want to come and play with us' Eddie asked James.
James was too busy turning the pages on the book.
'Maybe another time Eddie', but thank you' said Ross.
'James is very shy today'
He rubbed his fingers through James's hair.
'Ok' said Eddie and ran off to his friends.
Ross talked about his family and the accident.
'How old is James? asked Sarah.
'He will be four soon won't you James? Ross replied.
'They grow up quickly 'commented Gregg.
'Enjoy them whilst they are young'.
Ross was there an hour talking with them.
The time went by quickly.
'Well' said Ross 'I've taken up enough of your time',
It was nice to meet you both'.
'Not at all' it was nice meeting you too' said Gregg.'
'Come for a drink some other time and bring Laura.'
'Yes that would be nice' said Ross.
Ross thanked Sarah for the drinks.

'Goodbye James maybe you can come and play with Eddie some time', she said to him.

'You should ask him to get the toy cars out next time you visit.' She, told James.

'James say thank you to the lady for your drink?'

James held out his hand to Sarah.

'Thank you' he said to her.

'That's alright' you can come again, she said to him.

'Are you going now', asked Eddie, to Ross, as he walked to the gate.

'Yes', replied Ross 'It's James's lunch time bye for now'.

'See you again' Eddie, Sarah and Gregg.

With that, Ross left pleased, he had meet the neighbours.

'Where have you two been' asked Laura.

I was worried about you', she told Ross.

'James will be ready for his lunch'.

'Oh don't fuss Laura' replied Ross.

He told her all about Eddie and meeting his parents.

Laura was surprised when Ross said he had been invited in for a, coffee and enjoyed having a conversation with Greg and Sarah.

'They want us to have a drink with them some time' said Ross.

'The lady gave me some juice mummy' said James.

'That was very nice of her' she replied.

'I hope you said thank you to her' she asked.

'Of course he did' replied Ross.

'It would be nice to meet her' they sound like nice neighbours' replied, Laura',

Through the night Ross kept thinking about Eddie.

Those words 'my mum said' going round, and round, in his mind.

He jolted up in bed, sweating.

He knew he had to do something he couldn't carry on as he was.

Realising he had Laura and James to care for.

Also, aware of what Jimmy had said.

She had been a good wife to stick by him all this time.

Some wives would have walked away before now.

He didn't know how lucky he was.

What was he to do now?

His mind felt like it was going to burst.

He was so confused.

'Ross, whatever's the matter with you? Laura asked him as he sat up, in bed.

'Sorry to wake you Laura, I was just having a bad dream 'he replied.

'Seeing Jimmy brought it all back to me 'he explained.

He couldn't tell Laura the truth.

Pulling off the bed sheets, he said.

'I'm going down for a drink of water I won't be long'.

After breakfast Ross decided to phone the insurance company.

To see how they were getting on with the settlement for his accident.

They assured him they were doing everything they could to get a quick, outcome.

He knew when the money came through he could decide what he was, going to do with the future.

Laura had been the main provider financially for them.

Laura decided to phone Janet to let her know how Ross was doing.

Whilst they were talking she told her all about Ross meeting the new, neighbours.

She explained about their son Eddie.

'Well that a change' said Janet, 'do you think he's sorting himself, out'

''I don't know, but he does seem a bit more cheerful now days', replied Laura.

'Maybe he is 'I know it's not been easy for him'

'But time will tell she said.

Well I'm pleased for you both' replied Janet.

Chapter 38

The day came for Ross getting his payment from the Insurance, Company.

Although he knew it didn't compensate for what had happened, it would be a big help financially.

He had mixed feelings about it all.

What was he going to do now?

Ross put on his coat to go for a walk.

Opening the front door, he realised how he looked forward to his talks, with Eddie.

He strolled down the road taking in the morning air.

Whilst listening to the birds singing in the trees'.

The simple things in life he thought to himself.

He felt the freshness of the air on his face.

He would take a nice steady walk' have a talk to, Eddie, then go back, home to read the paper.

He had all the time in the world.

After all Laura wouldn't be home until after work, later that day.

Eddie was there as usual in the garden.

The young lad was trying to swing a golf club.

Each time he tried he lost his balance.

Ross stood and watched him whilst looking at every move.

After a time he walked up to Eddie he noticed that he had been crying.

Eddie slung the club down on the grass,

'I can't do it mister' he said to Ross

'Yes you can Eddie' said Ross positively.

'Remember what your mum says' you can do anything.'

'I know but this is harder' said Eddie

Come on now Eddie, it's not like you to give up' said Ross.

'Let me try and help you'.

Ross wondered what he was doing.

How can I show him he thought?

He had no grip in his hand.

How would he demonstrate if he couldn't do it himself?

Ross picked the club up from off the grass, and handed it to Eddie.

Ross was determined to help him.

'Look, let's see what we can do, there's a swing somewhere, let's see if we can find it' Ross told him.

With that, between them they worked on swinging the club and hitting, the ball.

After a while Ross looked at his watch.

The time had gone by so quickly.

'I have to go now Eddie' he said.

'You keep working on that swing'.

'Thanks Ross' replied Eddie.

'Will you come again tomorrow?' Eddie asked Ross.

'We'll see, maybe 'you take care' replied Ross.

With that Ross walked back home.

Wondering what had just happened.

He had helped Eddie for the first time.

It made him feel there was a purpose in life.

He had enjoyed every minute with him.

When Laura came home he told her the good news about the, settlement money.

'Great, now what are you going to do' she asked him.

I don't know' answered Ross.

'Well you could look for a new car, and then we'll see what work is, out there' she suggested.

That would come hard for Ross; he had been used to being his own, boss for so long.

'You know you can work for your dad' Laura told him.

'You would soon pick up the sales side of the job'.

He didn't want to rely on working in his dad's showroom.

He had no interest in selling cars.

'I'll see what is available and have a think about it' he told her.

'Let's look for a car I can drive first' he said.

'We'll you should get some help with disability' she told him.
'Sorry Ross, I didn't mean it to come out like that.
She soon said.
'I know, let's not talk about it anymore' replied Ross.
 With that Laura walked in to the kitchen to prepare a meal for them all.
 Ross was playing with James and his toy cars. .
His mind kept wandering to what skills he had apart from golfing?
James was getting annoyed with him.
 'Daddy you're not doing it right' said James.
You've parked them in the wrong place.
 'Sorry James how naughty of Daddy' he said laughing.
Just then Laura came to the rescue come on you two it's meal time'.
 Whilst they were eating their evening meal he told her about Eddie.
 Was she hearing right, She thought?
 Ross was helping Eddie with his golf swing.
 She could hardly believe what he was saying.
But underneath she felt happy for him.
 Ross helped her clear the table.
Laura got James ready for bed, then Ross read him a bedtime story.
 Laura was in her study, preparing some paperwork, to take into work,
the next day.
 What job could Ross find to help them all, she thought?
 He had his compensation.
 So there was no reason he couldn't start looking for work, after all he,
couldn't stay at home all day.
 The next day Charlie came as usual to do some gardening.
 Ross told him about getting his money and they talked about the,
future.
 What was he going to do with himself now?
 He had spent so much time around the house he was not sure of what,
was out there, and if he could even get work.
 Golf had been his life.
 Now he had to think about the future for them all.

Charlie didn't know what to say.

He knew that it had been hard for Ross to accept he couldn't play golf, anymore, with his injury to his arm.

Like him, he loved the time on the tournaments and travelling around, the world.

It had taken him to some beautiful places.

'Well you'll have to see what's out there you won't?' 'You will never, know until you try' said Charlie to him.

'Maybe you're right' replied Ross.

Charlie put the tools back in the shed.

'I'll be off then, I'll see you later in the week' Charlie said to him.

'Yes, and thanks Charlie' replied Ross.

'Bye then' he said then Charlie headed for home.

Chapter 39

Ross phoned Jimmy later that day and arranged to meet up,
 for a drink.
 Whilst on the phone he talked to Jimmy about getting the,
compensation, now he could buy a car.
 He would have to have the controls modified on a vehicle for him to,
drive.
 Since the accident he had relied on Laura to drive him most places he,
wanted to go to.
 Now, he thought, it was time for him to have a go at getting behind the,
wheel.
 He knew it wouldn't be easy for him as each time he got in the car the,
accident came flooding back to him.
 Although Laura was a steady driver he still felt edgy when he was in,
the passenger seat.
 Ross had been having physiotherapy to strengthen up his arm muscles.
 Due to his lack of movement in his hand he had no grip to hold a,
steering wheel.
He couldn't lift his arm due to the nerve damage.
 It would feel strange at first for him to drive
 When Laura came home Ross talked about going to look at some cars.
 'Well if that's what you want to do' she replied'
 You need to look for something that can be modified for,
you with your disability' said Laura.
 Ross snapped back at her, they already do that now on vehicles,
I'm not an invalid', he told her.
 I didn't say you were I'm only trying to help' she replied.
 Ross was annoyed she'd even thought about it.
 'Well please yourself' Ross she said, as she walked out the room
 'I can't win with you sometimes' she said angrily.

Ross didn't want to upset her he knew she meant well.

He followed behind her, 'sorry Laura I know you were only, trying to help' he said gently.

I'll sort it out.

Laura dropped Ross off at Jimmy's house on her way to work.

When Jimmy answered the door he said to Ross.

'You made it then, come in and have a seat I'll be ready in a minute'.

While Jimmy was getting ready Ross talked to him about what type, of car he had in mind.

'If you like, I can take you to your dad's garage, mentioned Jimmy,

Ross wasn't sure he was ready to get back in a car with Jimmy behind, the wheel.

I don't know, maybe I'll wait another day' said Ross.

'That's ok' said Jimmy 'I can understand'.

'Sorry Jimmy, I don't mean to sound ungrateful' he replied.

There was silence for a moment 'Jimmy I will take you up on the offer' he suddenly said to him.

'Are you sure Ross?' asked Jimmy' with a surprised look on, his face.

'Yes, come on, before I change my mind, Ross replied.

'Off we go then, 'said Jimmy.

Ross stood at the passenger side of Jimmy's car and hesitatingly, opened the car door.

'You alright Ross' asked Jimmy.

'You look a bit pasty.'

'No I'm fine let's go' Jimmy

Ross settled in the car, and put his seat belt on.

Jimmy reversed out the drive slowly on to the road then they were on, their way.

The thought of the accident went through Jimmy's mind,

Was Ross ever going to trust his driving again?

Although, he was in the passenger seat so that was a start.

Jimmy could see the tension in Ross face, so he drove carefully to the, garage.

They finally arrived at the garage.

Ross was pleased with himself.

He had made himself a challenge to get back in a car with Jimmy at, the, wheel and managed to do it.

'Thanks' Jimmy' he said.

Now let's see what they've got shall we.

Ross had come to terms more with his injuries.

He knew he could manage to drive a modified, automatic car.

He could get some help with disability.

With that, they both got out the car and headed for the showroom.

Phillip was pleased to see Ross and Jimmy.

It reminded him of their early years together.

Looking around Ross noticed that there were several choices.

He managed to find one he liked an automatic.

He discussed with his dad the modification needed with the steering, column for him to drive that would not cause discomfort to his injured, arm, and he could drive quite well.

Ross couldn't wait to get home to tell Laura all about it.

Ross got used to driving short trips with the car.

He felt it gave him some independence back, and didn't have to rely, on, Laura so much, which took the pressure off Laura.

He could now take himself to his appointments.

He searched online, looking for jobs that were of interest to him.

It was a minefield out there for work.

The days passed by and he was finding it frustrating trying to look, for a job.

There wasn't much out there suitable for him as he had limited, qualifications.

This made him more confused.

One day he switched off the computer.

Grabbed his coat off the hook and left the house.

He took a walk down the lane hoping to see Eddie.

He'd got used to having his daily chats with Eddie.

He was wondered how he was getting on with his golf.

He wondered how Eddie's could be so enthusiastic trying out new, things to do all the time.

But then he must have some depressing times, thought Ross.

Although Eddie was a young boy and children adapt better than grown, up some time thought Ross.

Eddie was always being encouraged by his mother.

Surely there must have been difficult times for her also.

His mind went to Laura.

How would he have managed without her?

He would never know that she was planning to leave him at one time.

As he walked by the house he noticed Eddie wasn't outside.

He wondered if he was ok.

Should he go to his house to enquire?

He may have gone out with his parents, thought Ross.

Ross didn't think the time would come when he would miss seeing, him in the garden.

He had got so used to Eddie being out their when he walked by.

It was if they both relied on seeing each other.

It felt strange to not see him and have a chat.

On returning home he had just got in the house when the phone rang'.

'Hello Ross, 'it's Jimmy' he said.

'I'm pleased I've caught you in'.

'I've got something to tell you, I thought you might be interested in'.

'What's that?' he asked Jimmy inquisitively.

'I'll pick you up, we can talk about it over a drink, said Jimmy.

'Sound mysterious Jimmy'? Answered Ross.

'Not really' I'll explain soon.

'I'm coming over now, get yourself ready'.

'Ok, 'sounds as though you've made my mind up for me' said Ross, laughing.

'Yes it does, 'so I'll see you soon' said Jimmy.

Ross was curious at what Jimmy was going to tell him.

What was all the mystery about?

The suspense was killing him.

Jimmy had another person with him in the car when he came to pick,
up Ross.

What's he up to he thought?

Ross got into the car.

'Ross meet Graham, he lives just outside the village' said Jimmy.
Ross said hello to Graham.

'Graham's dad owns the farm down the road' Jimmy explained.
Ross was wondering what Jimmy was doing.

Why Graham was in the car and what had this to do with Ross.

They arrived at the pub and found a table in a quiet corner.

Jimmy ordered a round of drinks for them all.

'I wanted you to meet Graham because he might have a position for,
you' if you're interested? Said Jimmy.

The plot thickened 'Oh and what might that be? Asked Ross.

"I think we've kept him in enough suspense", said Graham.

Graham took over the conversation, 'It's like this Ross'.

'I've been trying to get planning permission to turn some of the land,
the other end of town into a golf course and it's just been approved".

Ross listened intensively.

'What I'm looking for is someone in the know that I could rely on as,
a manager, especially as I'm away on tour a lot of the time.'

'I need someone who knows, and understands about golf.'

'When I mentioned it to Jimmy, straight away he suggested you Ross'.

'I thought, who better than Ross' said Jimmy butting in'.

Graham continued with the conversation.

'Maybe you would consider in investing in the project yourself?'

Ross was all ears, and the three men were their most of the day,
discussing the details.

"What amount of money would he consider investing", Ross asked,
himself.

If he did not invest then what amount of money is graham interested,
in paying someone to manage the estate while he was on tour.

Graham had looked thoroughly into it and knew the business would, benefit the town.

There were no good golf courses nearby.

The more he heard from graham, and thought about it, the more, interested he became.

Graham showed them the plans for the club house and including the, design of the course.

Ross was in his element the more they discussed it the more excited, underneath he became.

'I would need to discuss it with Laura' commented Ross to Graham.

'Of course Ross' I wouldn't expect it any other way' replied Graham.

'Have a good think about it, I'm sure you're the man for the job.

'With your experience, I think it could really work.

What about his disability what concern would that be to Graham.

Ross discussed everything with him but to Graham there was no, concerns after all , Ross would have plenty of staff to organize on the, premises what Graham wanted was someone with the knowledge, of golf and courses.

'Well that enough talking for today said graham, it's time I was going, home', they all agreed with him.

They finished their drinks and headed for the car.

Jimmy drove Ross home.

Ross thanked Graham and Jimmy for considering him.

This really had got Ross thinking on the way home.

He had his money from the insurance.

He also had his family to think about and couldn't afford to lose any, of it.

'Nice meeting you', Graham said to Ross as he got out the car.

'You to' replied Ross.

'Think about what I said Ross, and don't leave it to long before you, make up your mind' Graham told him.

'I won't, replied Ross, 'although I must say I'm more than interested, so I'll be in touch soon'.

'That what I was hoping to hear' replied Graham.

'Catch up tomorrow Ross' shouted Jimmy from the car window.

'Ok, and Thanks for today Jimmy' replied Ross.

Laura was already home when Ross walked in the door.

'I was wondering where you were?' she asked him, 'I phoned dad and he said he hadn't seen you.'

'Neither had your lot '

'Sorry love but, I've had a very interesting afternoon'. I didn't realise what the time was.'

'Jimmy rang and asked me to go for a drink'.

Ross told her all about the meeting with Graham.

'I don't know Ross it's a bit risky' she said anxiously.

'You know what it's like being in business these days',

'There are lots of facts to consider'.

'Has this Graham thought things through like when winter comes and, the course isn't busy', she asked.

'Well he said, he's got some other plans he's working on to bring in, the money for that time of year' said Ross.

'Let's think about, it before you go ahead with something you'll regret', she asked Ross.

Ross had more or less made his mind up even if Laura was cautious, about it all.

He would accept the manager's job and may be looking at investing, some of his money in shares in the club.

Chapter 40

Charlie came round the next day to do some gardening.
As it was Sunday Laura suggested he stayed for lunch.
Ross could talk to him about the offer he'd had to be manager,
of the golf club and the investment side.
With all her dad's experience it would do Ross good to discuss it with,
him thought Laura.
Charlie and Ross had a good conversation over lunch about the,
Golf course.
Charlie listening to what Ross had to say.
'What's your opinion' Ross asked Charlie?
'Well Ross', what do you want to do? Charlie asked him.
'I'd like to invest some money into it, and take the manager's job'
Ross replied.
'After all, I know all about courses and Golf' he continued.
'I think you'd make a good job of it' he said to Ross.
'So does Jimmy or he wouldn't have wanted you to meet Graham?'
'It could be a new beginning for you all'.
Over lunch they discussed the idea of Ross managing the golf course.
'Look Laura I'm not getting any younger' said Charlie.
I've got that big house, and I'm rattling about in on my own it will be,
yours one day'.
'So don't worry about money'.
'If this is what Ross wants then let's all pull together' he said.
'I'm sure this new golf course is a good Idea'.
'I'm sure things will work out, you'll see said Charlie.
'Oh dad, Laura started to cry'.
'Come on now love you'll have me in tears' laughed Charlie.
Now let's finish lunch then we can take James for a walk he suggested.

When the time came for Charlie to leave Ross put his arm around him.
'Thank you for today Charlie, he said to him.
I appreciate all the help and support you've given us' said Ross.
'I know you do' replied Charlie.
'Let me know how the next meeting goes with your friend?
Asked Charlie.
'I will' Ross told him'.
   The next week Ross met up with Graham and Jimmy to discuss in,
more details about the golf course.
 They discussed the design and costing, not only for the course but also,
for the club house.
  This was something they all knew they had to get right.
 It would take time before it would be up and running.
 There was the drainage to think of, around the course.
 But they all knew it would not come without its problems.
 They also had to make sure it paid for itself.
The wanted to use the function room for social events.
This would bring in more revenue.
 It would provide employment for local people as well as outsiders.
 Ross and Jimmy both decided to invest in some shares.
 Ross couldn't afford to lose out financially.
   Although he felt nervous about it, his intuition told him he was doing,
the right thing.
 He would also be taking on the manager's job.
 Graham knew Ross would put all his years of experience in to the,
running of it all.
 There was so much to discuss they had arranged another meeting.
Graham and jimmy would be off on tour.
 Graham would be leaving Ross to deal with the project whilst he was,
away.
 The paper work for shares in the club would be made available for,
Ross and Jimmy to sign on Graham's return.
 They raised their glasses to new adventure.

After lots of talking, and several pints they decided to call it a day, they shook hands and said their goodbyes for the night.
 Ross still couldn't believe this was happening.

The months went by the leaflets had been sent out to different locations, advertising the open day.
 Full page adverts were put in the paper and Golfing Magazines.
 Ross wondered how many people would turn up,
The local press would be there.
 Also some journalists were attending, they wanted to see some of the, professional players who were arriving to support Graham.
 It would be like old times for Ross, catching up with some of them, thought Jimmy.
 Jimmy had sent out the invite to some top players to encourage more, people to come and encourage advertising.
 There was one person Ross knew he couldn't leave out.
 His mind went straight to Eddie he would speak to his parents.

Talking to Laura three weeks before about it, they both decided to, throw a party for the neighbour's and invite a few friends.
Laura had sent out some invites.
 On the morning of the party Ross had organized a firm to come to put, up the marquee in the garden
Charlie came round early to assist.
 Mary had taken James to town to collect some items.
Josie was busy helping Laura with the food.
 Jimmy and Ross went to get the beer and wine and an assortment of, soft drinks.
 'That was just up Jimmy's street' commented Ross.
 Who else could they rely on to do the job so well?
 The afternoon went well, everyone was enjoying themselves.
Some friends had brought their children along, to play with James.
 Ross had arranged a bouncy castle for them to play on.
 Graham flirted with one of Laura's friends from work.
Just like Jimmy' Josie thought laughing.

She could see why they got on well.

Eddie came with his parents.

James had lots of fun on the bouncy castle and playing with the toy, cars with Eddie.

Phillip had made him a two tier garage with a mechanics ramp.

He loved playing with it, putting the cars on the ramp pressing the, button and up it went.

He made a car wash, and put in some petrol pumps.

Ross told his dad he could make some money if he patented it.

The afternoon went well with everyone.

The guests commented on the food, how delicious it tasted and what a, good spread they had put on.

Everyone enjoyed themselves.

Ross spoke to Eddie's parents, and explained that he had been an, inspiration to Ross, and had inspired them to the opening of the course.

He wanted to talk to the crowd about Eddie, if they agreed?

After all, it was through seeing him trying everyday and not giving up, that had helped him see things differently.

They were overwhelmed this would mean the world to Eddie and, they thought it was wonderful that Ross had thought so much of him.

You'll be there then?' he asked them.

If Eddie had his way he'd be sleeping there the night before so he, wouldn't miss anything' said his parents.

Ross laughed' I think you may be right' he replied.

The day came for the grand opening of the Golf Course.

Ross stirred early showered then went down for breakfast.

After breakfast he took a walk down the drive to collect the post.

When he opened the box there in the pile of letter there was one from, the hospital.

Ross looked surprised, when he opened the letter.

It was from, Mr Turner the consultant.

He was requesting Ross to make an appointment to see him, regarding some new development in micro chip implants.

Ross stood there reading it for several minutes then showed the letter to Laura.

'I wonder what that's all about' he asked her.

'How would I know,' she said.

'I think you should phone to arrange an appointment to see him".

"He obviously wants to see you or why else would he write to you',
she told Ross.

Ross phoned Mr.Turner's secretary to arrange an appointment,
but didn't want to get his hopes up.

Underneath though he was hoping it would be to his advantage in,
new technology after all they were advancing in new medical science,
daily.

It was a big day for them all the opening of the Golf Course.
Crowds of people came from miles around.
The local band would be playing.

Graham walked up to the microphone and gave it a tap to see if it,
was switched on and everyone could hear him.

'One two three' One two three he said down the microphone.

'Come on Graham, Jimmy shouted to him.

'You're not doing a dance.'
Graham looked down at his golf shoes.

'Not in these shoes' he said.

The crowd laughed.

Now he knew it was working he could begin.

'Welcome everyone, and thank you for coming to our,
'Grand opening day'.

It's good to see so many people here' he said.

'We are very excited about today and about the golf course'.

He introduced the professional players to the guests.
Who had made the journey, not only had they been his,
opposition in the competitions over the years also his friends off the,
course.

They were proud off his inspiration to build his own golf course.

The support they gave him was credit to them all.

They laughed when Graham said he would get in a few free rounds, off golf.

He talked a little about himself and how he came to the idea of golf, course.

'It must have been when Jimmy and I were having a late night, drinking session' commented graham.

'I couldn't remember much the next morning'.

'I just know that I looked at the napkin stuffed in my trouser, pocket the next morning, and wondered what the drawings were about, then it clicked' he explained.

The crowd howled with laughter.

Ross's mind went back to Trout Valley.

That's about right he thought Jimmy and his late night drinking.

For one moment his mind flashed back to the letter from

Mr. Turner.

Graham stood for a few seconds

Graham carried on saying 'of course there is one person who a lot of, you already know' 'Ross Portland.

Graham put his hand on Ross's shoulder.

'This man was champion golfer many times.

But due to unforeseen circumstances his life took a different path'.

'But that path was our gain' continued Graham.

When life changes direction who knows where it will take you? He said.

'In the short time I have got to know Ross'.

'I have all the confidence this will be a success, thanks to him'.

'After all he does have an investment in it he said laughing'.

'Jimmy, well what can I say about him?'

I have known Jimmy for a long time' he said.

'Let me tell you folks he doesn't change'.

'Mind you' Josie his future wife will keep him in line isn't that right, Jimmy' Jimmy just smiled.

Seriously folks, he's a good friend and I know he will give, Ross his support'.

The lads clapped and cheered for Jimmy.

Graham went on to say.

We hope this will also brings the community together.

The club will be used for social events.

He went on to say what competitions they had lined up.

There would not only be men's and ladies, but also mixed matches.

'Maybe some of the ladies would like to come to our range nights, we will be setting up?'

'Try your hand at golfing you might surprise yourself.

'Well that's enough from me' he said.

'I would now like to introduce to you the person who will be in, charge of everything' Ross Portland.

I have much faith in him; Graham said.

Graham stepped down and Ross took the stand.

'Thank you Graham for your support' said Ross.

He started by saying how pleased he was to have been given this, opportunity.

He explained a little about his accident, and how he came to meet, Graham.

He told them about his family and all the support they had given to, him.

Ross paused for a second, and then followed by saying.

Sometime things happen in life you can't understand.

At the time it's hard to ask why.

But who know what changes lay ahead for us all.

There is one other person here today whom I give credit too and this, young lad who I admire.

He hesitated for a second and looked at Eddie.

He looked into the crowd and proceeded to say.

'When I went for my daily walks, and still do down the lane,
where I live I would meet this young lad'.

'He would always be out there trying, to play football, cricket or golf'.

'Although he had his problem with his leg he never gave up'.

'He was an inspiration'.

'On my daily walk we would always stop and talk.'

'In fact he persistently made sure I talked to him' the crowd laughed.

'His favourite saying was and is'.

'My mum said'' my mum said you can do this,' my mum said you can, do that.'

'My mum said you can do anything if you try' he always told me.

'And try he did' smiled Ross.

'Those words went round in my head when I was coming to terms, with my disability'.

'I would like you all to meet this young lad'.

'Eddie' if you would like to come up here'.

Eddie walked on to the platform smiling, beaming from ear to ear.
The crowd noticed as he walked up to Ross he had some disability.
Ross put his arm around his shoulders.

'Give him a round of applause? Asked Ross.

They all clapped and cheered for Eddie.

Ross went on to say 'because of this young man we will be, setting up a group for people with disabilities'.

'Who would like to try playing golf?'

'We will have a personal coach for them.'

'I'm sure Eddie's name will be first on the list?

'You bet' said Eddie.

This will be our charity to help raise money for those like Eddie, to try and encourage them in to sports.

He turned to Eddie's parents and said' you must be very proud of, Eddie'.

'As we all are' he said.

Ross also thanked Jimmy for all his help.

After all if it wasn't for him recommending him to Graham, he would not be standing here today.

'Well all I can say now is take a look around and enjoy the food and, drinks'.

'Have a good time everyone' ended Ross.

Ross stepped down from the platform.

'Well done' said Laura 'I'm proud of you' as she gave him a kiss.

Ross smiled at Laura and gave James a hug; he knew everything was, going to be alright.

He turned around, rubbed his hand through Eddie's hair and said to, him.

'By the way what was that saying?

The End.

Jane Darnes lives in Peterborough.

Her son and daughter in law, and two Granddaughter's live in Bourne. Her daughter and son in law Granddaughter and Grandson live in Zimbabwe.

I would like to thank my Daughter for her assistance with my book.

Printed in Great Britain
by Amazon